Praise for the *Out of Uniform* series

"I'm so glad I discovered this series."
— Mandi Schreiner, *USA TODAY*

"I love this erotic series by Elle Kennedy. Featuring Navy SEAL heroes and the women who tame them ..."
— *Smexy Books*

"...a delight to read...funny yet natural. I think Elle Kennedy books should have a tagline that says something like 'She gives good dialogue'."
— *Dear Author*

"Each story I pick up by Kennedy has me falling further and further in love with her writing. She has quickly become one of my favorite go-to authors for a sexy good time!"
— *Book Pushers*

"You can always count on Elle Kennedy to bring the sexy times. There are plenty of steamy scenes and the romantic build up starts early on and just keeps on building."
— *Fiction Vixen*

Also available from Elle Kennedy

Out of Uniform
Hot & Bothered
Hot & Heavy

Off-Campus
The Deal
The Mistake
The Score
The Goal

Outlaws
Claimed
Addicted
Ruled

***

A full list of Elle's print titles is available on her website
www.ellekennedy.com

Hot & Bothered

Out of Uniform

Elle Kennedy

Copyright

Author's Note

I am SO excited to be re-releasing the *Out of Uniform* series! For those of you who haven't read it before, this was one of my earlier series, and it also happens to be one of my favorites, probably because this is when I realized how much I love writing bromances!

Seriously. The boy banter in these books still cracks me up to this day. You see more and more of it as the series progresses, and by the later books there are entire chapters of crazy conversations between my sexy, silly SEALs.

For new readers, you should know that a) you don't have to read the stories in order, though characters from previous books do show up in every installment. And b) the first six stories are novellas (20-35,000 words), while the last four are full-length novels (80,000+ words).

I decided to release the novellas as two books featuring three stories each (*Hot & Bothered, Hot & Heavy*) making the total books in the series SIX rather than the original ten.

***IMPORTANT**: These books have NOT changed, except for some minor editing and proofreading. There are grammatical differences and some (minor) deleted/added lines here and there, but for the most part, there is *no new content*. If you've previously purchased and read *Heat of the Moment, Heat of Passion* and *Heat of the Storm*, then you won't be getting anything new with *Hot & Bothered*, aside from a gorgeous new cover!

Fun facts:

- *Heat of the Moment* is the shortest because it was only supposed to be a short story in an anthology that the series' previous publisher had released. I never intended on writing more books, but readers fell in love with Carson, the secondary character, and demanded he get his own story. But when I wrote *Heat of Passion*, I made the mistake of introducing other members of the SEAL team—and I fell in love with each and every one of them. Which meant *they* needed their own stories, too, and there you have it—a 10-book series was born!

- *Heat of the Moment* also features my original use of the name Garrett! Absolutely NO relation or similarities to Garrett Graham of *Off-Campus* fame, but I loved the name so much I decided to use it again.

So, I hope you enjoy the new cover, the better grammar, and the hot, dirty-talking SEALs who to this day hold such a big place in my heart!

Love,

Elle

Heat of the Moment

An Out of Uniform Novella

Elle Kennedy

Chapter One

Why was it that heat waves always made her want to have sex? Shelby Harper wasn't certain, but she suspected it had something to do with the spike of body temperature and the constant sheen of sweat that coated her body, clinging to her breasts, sticking to her legs. It made her want to rip her clothes off and wander around naked until the end of time. And thinking about being naked logically led to thoughts of sex, right?

Or hell, maybe it wasn't the heat wave at all. Maybe she really shouldn't have taken the tequila shot that cute Navy lieutenant had tempted her into. But she'd never been able to say no to a man in uniform...

Too bad the guy was married. He really was appealing, with his clean-shaven jaw and those playful green eyes.

Fighting a smile, Shelby reached for another ice cube from the plastic cup sitting on the smooth countertop. Though most of the ice had already melted, she managed to find one cube still intact, and slowly ran it over her collarbone. The ice felt heavenly against her fevered skin. A cold shower might have felt even nicer, but she'd already taken one this morning and she was trying to conserve energy.

"Jesus, Shel, turn on the air conditioning. I'm dying of heat here," a sexy male voice drawled.

The ice cube slid out of her fingers and down her shirt, landing directly in the left cup of her lacy pink bra. Her nipple instantly hardened, though it was hard to tell if it was a result of the ice or the sight of John Garrett standing in front of the bakery counter.

When had he come in here? Her shop was divided into a bakery and a café, the latter being where most of the customers had holed up all evening. She hadn't even noticed John—no, he liked to be called Garrett, she reminded herself—she hadn't noticed *Garrett* walk into the bakery. Not surprising, since he was a Navy SEAL and possessed the eerie ability to make himself invisible until he decided to materialize out of nowhere.

At the moment, however, he was the furthest thing from invisible. Wearing a pair of olive-green cargo pants that hugged his long, muscular legs and a white T-shirt that was pasted to his rock-hard abs thanks to the heat, he was really, *really* visible. He shot her a grin that was even sexier than that husky voice of his, adding, "I'm hot."

Oh yes you are…

She quickly silenced the naughty voice inside her head. Yes, Garrett was hot—he was the walking, talking and breathing definition of tall, dark and handsome. And yes, his body was to die for, with all those perfectly sculpted muscles that didn't come from a gym but from swimming with sharks and hanging off helicopters—or whatever it was he did as a SEAL. But no matter how good he looked, she knew fantasizing about this man would get her nowhere.

Garrett wasn't interested in her. A year of flirting and that one pathetic attempt she'd made at asking him out to dinner confirmed this sad truth. Whether she liked it or not, he'd apparently tucked her away in friend territory. Which was probably a good thing, because did she really want to hook up with Garrett anyway? She'd played the part of military girlfriend before, and look how well *that* turned out. Not only had Matthew, her ex, been away for months at a time, but he'd been doing more than playing GI Joe when he was gone—he'd been fucking every female he happened to encounter.

"Earth to Shelby."

She lifted her head and saw Garrett was still standing there, still staring at her. Jeez, this heat was making her space out.

"Sorry, what did you want?"

"Air conditioning," he prompted.

"Forget it."

"Come on," he said with another grin, and then a wink. Man, how did he get away with *winking*? Most men looked like complete idiots when they tried to wink. "Give me five minutes in front of the air conditioner, full blast, just to cool off."

"Increased use of air conditioning during heat waves causes power outages," she reminded him. "Which is why half the city is experiencing a blackout. I'd rather be all sweaty than without power for five days."

She was pretty grateful, actually, that her bakery was the only place in a ten-mile radius that had power, all thanks to the backup generator she'd decided to switch on. No way was she going to put a strain on the genny by cranking the A/C. She hated using it as it was, but she had an entire refrigerator full of cakes that needed to be delivered tomorrow morning and she'd be damned if all those cakes spoiled because John Garrett wanted a little bit of cold air. She'd already done him and his Navy buddies a favor by opening the café on a Sunday evening. The lit-up front window drew the men like flies to honey. To them, electricity meant television, and television meant the ability to see the big game between the Padres and the Dodgers.

He lifted a brow. "You're all sweaty, huh?"

Figured he'd latch onto that one teeny part of her response.

"Yes, Garrett, I'm sweaty. It's a billion degrees out there, in case you've forgotten."

"Which only supports my idea about the air conditioning."

"Forget it." She set her jaw and crossed her arms over her chest to show she meant business. "Find another way to cool off."

A loud cheer came from the adjoining room, followed by the sound of palms slapping against palms in high-fives. The Padres had obviously scored another run.

"The game's almost done. You could take a quick dip in the ocean after you leave here," she said, trying to be helpful.

But Garrett didn't seem to be interested in cooling methods anymore. His chocolate-brown eyes glittered with a mixture of amusement and curiosity as he studied her chest. "Are you...uh, lactating?"

Huh?

She quickly glanced down, suppressing a groan when she saw the water stain that had seeped from her bra right through her thin yellow tank top.

"Ice," she blurted out.

"Pardon me?"

"An ice cube fell down my shirt."

He gave a husky little laugh that made her nipples harden again. Damn it. Everything about this man was way too appealing. His warrior body, his messy dark hair and teasing eyes, his laughter. She'd been attracted to Garrett from the second he'd sauntered into her bakery last year to buy a cake for his commander's birthday. He'd requested the most obscene message to be written in icing, and from that moment on, she was a goner.

Maybe she was through with dating military men, but she knew that all John Garrett had to do was ask and she'd have her clothes off in a nanosecond.

But he didn't ask. He *never* asked. In the year she'd known him Garrett hadn't shown one iota of interest in getting naked with her.

"You should take off your shirt."

Until now.

She managed a startled laugh. "Really? Why is that?"

His smile was boyishly innocent. "Because it's all wet. Or, if you'd prefer, I could get a couple more of those ice cubes and rub them over your right breast. You know, so you match."

She laughed again, this time to cover up the zing of arousal she'd just felt at the words "rub" and "your" and "breast" coming out of this man's sexy mouth. He was obviously joking around. He had to be. Because although she'd imagined Garrett's hands on her breasts countless times before, she knew the fantasy would forever stay in her imagination.

If John Garrett wanted her, he'd have made a move a long time ago.

So instead of responding to his flirty remark, she said, "You'll miss the end of your game."

Something that resembled disappointment flickered in his dark eyes. "Yeah." He coughed. "You're right. I should, ah, head back in there. Sorry I came in here and bugged you."

What? He thought he was bugging her?

She opened her mouth to tell him he could hang out with her a bit longer, that she wasn't trying to shoo him away, but he turned around before she could say a word. She got a glimpse of his taut backside disappearing through the doorway leading into the café and then he was gone.

Well.

Shelby leaned her elbows on the counter and rested her flushed face in her hands. What exactly just happened here?

She replayed the entire scene in her mind, starting with the way Garrett had walked in and demanded she turn on the air conditioner and ending with his offer to *rub* her breasts. And then, of course, his abrupt departure.

Had she done something wrong? Maybe she hadn't flirted enough? She would have flirted more, but she hadn't seen the point. She'd tried it before, and Garrett always brushed off her suggestive remarks, making it obvious he wasn't interested but never making her feel as if she were inadequate or anything. He genuinely seemed to like her, but after a year of friendship it was clear he wasn't into her the way she was into him.

"You don't want to get involved with him anyway," she muttered to herself.

The reminder helped, but only a little. Yeah, she wasn't interested in dating an officer again, but…but damn it, she really wished John Garrett would have sex with her.

"Another shot for our lovely hostess?"

She looked up and found Paul, the married lieutenant, by the counter—yet again holding the tequila bottle and a shot glass in his hands.

He was obviously trying to get her drunk, and she wondered if she ought to tell him that no amount of tequila would convince her to sleep with a married man. Nah. He'd find out soon enough, especially if he did something stupid, like grope her. If he did that, then he'd also find out she was pretty damn good at kicking him in the balls.

"I'm already feeling tipsy," she admitted, eyeing the bottle warily.

"Tipsy, shmipsy! It's the first heat wave of the summer! It's a special occasion."

Had he just said *tipsy shmipsy?*

Trying not to laugh, Shelby tucked her hair behind her ears. "No thanks, I'll pass." She couldn't go home until the Padres game ended, but drinking herself stupid was no way to pass the time until everyone left.

And it wasn't like another drink would help her forget that John Garrett, her long-time fantasy, was in the other room, *not* wanting to sleep with her.

No amount of tequila could make her forget *that*.

"FACE IT, SHE'S JUST NOT INTO YOU," CARSON SCOTT SAID WITH A SHRUG.

Garrett forced his gaze to stay glued on the television and not drift in the direction of the doorway separating the café from the bakery. His peripheral vision caught a flash of movement—Shelby rounding the counter to chat with Lieutenant Paul Aston and his tequila bottle.

Ha. Did Lieutenant Asshole actually think he had a flying fuck of a chance of getting Shelby Harper into bed? Dream on, brother.

Shelby would never mess around with a married man. Or at least that's what Garrett kept telling himself.

Because in all honesty, the thought of his sweet, sexy Shelby burning up the sheets with Lieutenant Asshole, or any man for that matter, caused jealousy to spiral down his chest and seize his intestines like a death vise.

"You might as well quit pining over the girl," Carson added, lifting his beer bottle to his mouth and taking a long swig.

"I'm not pining," Garrett said defensively. "I'm just..." His voice drifted, his brain unable to come up with an alternative description for the way he felt about Shelby.

Fuck. Fine. Maybe he *was* pining, just a little. But who could blame him? Shelby was pretty fricking amazing. Look up the definition of *sexy California girl* in the dictionary and Shelby Harper's picture would be there—her wavy, sun-streaked blonde hair, her big blue eyes with those incredibly long eyelashes, and the slender athletic body she kept in shape by surfing at Coronado Beach every morning.

Most of the Navy guys who met her thought she was the typical West Coast blonde, complete with the dumb part, but Garrett had only needed five minutes with the woman to know she was the furthest thing from dumb *and* typical.

Shelby Harper was smart as hell. Funny as hell. Nice as hell.

And there wasn't a chance *in* hell that she'd ever get naked with a guy like him.

"Look," Carson said after Garrett's silence had lasted a bit too long. "You've spent the last year acting like a choirboy, coming in here whenever you're on leave and buying those fancy-pants mocha latte Frappuccinos without ever telling Shelby that what you *really* want is to get inside her pants."

"You can't tell a woman like Shelby you want inside her pants," Garrett replied with a frown. He took a slow sip of his beer, but the liquid was already room temperature, and room temperature meant about ninety degrees. He forced himself to swallow the tepid beer, then pushed the bottle away.

"Why the hell not? She fills out a pair of pants pretty fucking nicely."

She sure did...

He forcibly shoved all thoughts of Shelby's tight ass out of his head. "I can't treat Shel the way I treated all the SEAL groupies I hooked up with. She's...classy and...*nice*. She deserves more than a couple sleazy come-ons."

"Well, since you've been striking out since day one, maybe a couple sleazy come-ons are what you need."

"I, uh, kinda tried that," he admitted. "Just now." A groan rose in his throat. "I offered to fondle her tits and she—"

Carson hooted. "You did *what*?"

"—pretty much ordered me to get out of her sight," he finished.

And now...now she was cozying up to Aston, who was clearly trying to get her drunk enough so she wouldn't care if he was married or not.

"Look, although the fondling line is gold," Carson chuckled again, "maybe it's time you accepted the fact that she's not interested. And do you blame her? This place is right near the base. Think of all the Navy personnel—and groupies—who come in here. She's probably heard all about your reputation, man."

Garrett clenched his teeth, fighting the urge to hit something, but deep down he knew Carson had a point. He was by no means a saint, and Shelby had undoubtedly heard some stories about him, most of them true.

At best, she knew his past was a revolving door of women. Lots of women. At worst, she was aware of his wild streak. Maybe even the threesomes, some with none other than Carson Scott, the guy sitting right beside him.

But his reputation was the reason he'd tried taking a different approach when it came to Shelby. He hadn't been overly flirtatious, hadn't acted disrespectfully, and he certainly hadn't made it obvious just how badly he wanted her naked beneath him while he drove his cock inside her and made her scream his name while she came…

Shit, definitely not a good idea to be thinking about stuff like that. He was already hot enough thanks to this heat wave.

Next to him, Carson wasn't finished with his lecture. "Shelby's not a wild chick, Garrett. You said it yourself—she's nice, wholesome, you know, the kind of woman who'd probably freak out if you suggested, I don't know, trying something other than the missionary position. She's got a body that won't quit, sure, but there's this whole innocent schoolgirl thing going on there. Maybe it's the freckles."

"I like the freckles."

"Yeah, me too. But I'm telling you, women with freckles are ridiculously vanilla when it comes to sex. I speak from experience, man."

Garrett laughed. "Let me guess, your little black book has an entire section reserved for freckle-faced women."

The other man just grinned, which made Garrett wonder if Carson really did categorize his conquests… Nah, even Carson wasn't that sleazy.

His brain stumbled over the word *sleazy*, and he had to wonder if that's how Shelby saw him. He hoped not, but he wouldn't be surprised if she did. Even though he'd bid goodbye to his wild ways, his reputation *did* precede him. So did his rep as SEAL, though Shel didn't seem all that impressed with his line of work. Most women were ready to rip their clothes off when they found out he was a big bad SEAL, an all-American hero. Yet he got the feeling Shelby viewed his job as a turn-off. He knew she'd dated a Marine a couple years ago and that the relationship had ended badly, so he'd always made a point not to talk about his work. Not that it helped. Seemed like nothing he did impressed the woman.

"You don't want to have sex with Shelby Harper," Carson was saying, still sipping on his beer.

Garrett rolled his eyes. "Cuz she has freckles?"

"That, and she's too fucking sweet. She's definitely not the type who'd be uninhibited in the bedroom." Carson laughed. "Can you ever see her going for kinky sex, or hell, a threesome? Shit, I'd love to be in the room and see her face if you ever suggested something like that."

A cheer echoed through the café. Garrett shifted his head and saw a couple of petty officers high-fiving over another run from the Padres.

Not interested in the game, he turned his gaze back to Carson, but not before he caught another flicker of movement from the corner of his eye. He quickly glanced at the doorway leading to the bakery, but it was empty.

Okay. He could've sworn he'd seen a flash of yellow—Shelby's clingy little tank top maybe?—but when he peered into the next room, he saw she was by the counter, still chatting with Lieutenant Asshole.

Another wave of jealousy slammed into him, even fiercer than the first. Goddammit. He hated the raw emotion that Shelby, with her vivid blue eyes and mouthwatering body, evoked inside him. It killed him how much he wanted her. All she had to do was bat those long lashes in his direction, give him the slightest hint that she was interested, and he'd be by her side in an instant. No, screw *by her side*. One word—and the word was *yes*—and he'd be so deep inside her pussy that neither of them would be able to walk again for days.

The thought made his cock twitch.

He needed to get out of here. If it weren't a million degrees out there, he might have left. Gone home, taken a quick dip in his condo's pool and slid into bed. But spending the rest of the night in the dark, sweating out this heat wave, was seriously unappealing. Shelby's café was the only place with power. Besides, as annoying as it was watching her with another man, at least he could keep an eye on her while he was here. Make sure she didn't get plastered and do something stupid. Like the lieutenant.

Yeah, that's why you're sticking around, a small voice taunted.

Fine, so maybe a part of him was hoping Shelby would get plastered and do *him*.

A guy could dream, right?

Chapter Two

CAN YOU EVER SEE HER GOING FOR KINKY SEX, OR HELL, A THREESOME?

Shelby kept running the words over and over again in her head, wondering if she'd somehow imagined them. It was hard enough to think in this sweltering heat—add to that a shot of tequila and you got one struggling-to-function brain.

But no, she couldn't have imagined it. She'd heard Garrett and Carson, loud and clear, as they'd discussed her. Scratch that—as they'd discussed all the reasons to *not* have sex with her.

It was quite insulting that they'd been locker-room talking about her in *her* place of business. And yet a part of her was...flattered.

Jeez, what was wrong with her? How could she possibly be flattered by the fact that Garrett and his buddy thought she was *vanilla*?

At least it answered the question she'd been asking herself this past year. Why didn't John Garrett want her? Well, because apparently she wasn't wild enough for him.

Oh, she knew he liked her. He'd made that pretty clear during his chat with Carson. But he'd also made it clear that he thought she was sweet. Not sweet, as in "man, she's got a sweet ass" but sweet as in "I don't want to fuck her because she's obviously a huge prude in the sack".

"I am *not* a prude," she mumbled.

"What was that, hon?"

Her head jerked up and she realized Paul was beside her again. "Oh. Nothing. I didn't say anything," she lied, suddenly wishing this man would just disappear.

One of the other officers was throwing up in the café restroom, so she'd let the lieutenant use the bathroom in the upstairs apartment, where she'd lived for the past two years. Paul's absence had allowed her to eavesdrop on Garrett's conversation, but now she kind of wished she'd never been nosy enough to lurk in the doorway. The last thing a woman wanted to hear was that the man she had the hots for didn't think she was *wild* enough for him.

"So what do you say we kick all these losers out and go upstairs?"

Okay, maybe *that* was the last thing a woman wanted to hear.

She shot the lieutenant a pointed look. "What would your wife have to say about that?"

He looked startled for a moment, then glanced down at the gold wedding band on his left hand as if remembering it was there.

Uh, yeah, buddy, maybe take the ring off before you try to hit on a woman who isn't your wife.

"My wife and I are actually separated," Paul said quickly.

Yeah right.

"I'm sure the separation must be very painful for you," Shelby said politely.

"So, the going upstairs idea…" He looked at her with a hopeful expression.

She just stared at him.

The hope dissipated like a puff of smoke. "Right." He shrugged. "Can't blame a guy for trying."

She opened her mouth to retort that, yes, she *could* blame a guy for trying, especially a *married* one, but he scurried off before she could speak.

Trying not to roll her eyes, Shelby watched as Paul ambled into the café, muttered something to the officer he'd arrived with, then left her establishment without a backwards glance.

"Jerk," she muttered under her breath.

"Please tell me you had something to do with Lieutenant Asshole running off like that." Carson Scott appeared in the doorway, a broad grin on his face.

"You guys call him Lieutenant Asshole?" she said with a laugh.

"Either that or Sleazebag Paul. It's hard to pick one, seeing as he's both an ass and a sleaze. We tend to alternate."

Shelby peered past Carson's impossibly broad shoulders, trying to catch a glimpse of Garrett. Apparently the game was over, because most of the men in the other room were pushing back their chairs and heading for the door. A few approached the doorway to thank her for opening up the bakery. She just smiled, waved and wondered where the hell Garrett had run off to. Probably to find a woman who was into kinky sex and threesomes.

Too bad. Because if he'd ever bothered to ask her, he might be surprised to learn that she was *exactly* that kind of woman. Just because she'd never acted out any of her fantasies didn't mean she didn't have 'em.

"So we're taking off," Carson was saying. "But we thought we'd help you clean up a little before we left. Garrett took the beer bottles out to the recycling bin. I came in here to get a rag so I could wipe down the tables."

She was genuinely touched. "You guys don't have to do that."

"It's the least we could do. You didn't have to open the café tonight, but you did. Might as well repay you with some clean-up."

He shot her a crooked smile, and a flicker of heat sparked inside her belly. Carson really was an attractive man, she realized. She'd been lusting over Garrett for so long she'd barely noticed what any of his friends looked like. Now, she actually took the time to look at Carson Scott, really *look* at him. And she definitely liked what she saw.

Dirty blond hair, cut short but not short enough that he looked like all the crew cut boys who walked around Coronado. His eyes were blue, his features classically handsome, and he was as ripped as his friend Garrett. Obviously you couldn't be a Navy SEAL without possessing one of those hard, sleek bodies that never failed to make a girl drool.

"Do I have icing on my chin or something?" Carson teased. "Damn, I knew I shouldn't have eaten one of those cupcakes you brought out to us."

"No, nothing on your chin," she said, cheeks warm as she turned away and stopped checking him out.

She rounded the counter and grabbed a rag, then handed it to him. Trying not to stare at his ass, she trailed him into the café and watched as he efficiently wiped down all the tabletops. Carson had just finished when Garrett returned, the chimes over the door jingling as he walked inside.

Shelby's heart immediately did a couple of jumping jacks. Damn it. Why did John Garrett always manage to make her pulse race?

"Thanks for having us." Garrett's voice was slightly gruff.

"No problem." She swallowed when she saw him edge back toward the door. She was suddenly anxious for him not to leave.

She still couldn't believe he thought she was vanilla, and maybe it was crazy—fine, it *was* crazy—but she got the feeling a golden opportunity was staring her square in the eye. That tonight would be her one chance to show him that she wasn't the sweet, freckle-faced prude he obviously thought she was.

"Well…good night," he said.

Their gazes locked, and she could swear the air hissed and crackled with mutual attraction.

Fine, it was probably the heat making the crackling noise, but still…

She broke the eye contact and slowly glanced over at Carson, who'd dropped the rag on one of the tables and was moving toward his friend.

Don't let them leave.

The urgent voice inside her head caught her off-guard, but only for a second. Because after that second was up, she realized she really *was* looking at a golden opportunity. A delicious, ridiculously tempting opportunity.

She's too fucking sweet. She's definitely not the type who'd be uninhibited in the bedroom.

God, it would be so wickedly satisfying to prove them wrong. Show Garrett that his kinks didn't scare her and that she was perfectly capable of taking him on. Taking them *both* on.

Heat simmered in her belly, radiated in her limbs and made her weak with…lust. Oh God. She'd always imagined what it would be like. Two men. At the same time. The guys she'd dated in the past would have been appalled if she admitted to that particular fantasy. Even Matthew, who'd seen nothing wrong with sleeping around on her, would have been horrified.

Was she crazy? Perverted? Suffering from heat stroke?

Maybe, but who the heck cared? They were all adults here. And yeah, maybe she was a little tipsy from the tequila, but like Lieutenant Asshole had said, tipsy shmipsy. What was so wrong with acting wild and crazy every now and then?

If wild was what she needed to be to show Garrett she could rock his world, then why not?

"See you later, Shel," Carson said.

Garrett's hand was on the doorknob.

"It's still early," she found herself blurting. "You guys should stay and hang out a while longer."

His hand froze as he glanced at her over his shoulder. "You want us to stay?"

She managed a feeble shrug. "Sure. Sleazebag Paul left his tequila bottle here. We might as well put it to good use."

Both men just stared at her, but Garrett's hand *did* drop from the door handle…

"Besides," she added, "it's so hot out there."

"Pretty hot in here, too," she heard Carson murmur.

She met Garrett's gorgeous brown eyes and offered a little smile. "So. What do you say?"

GARRETT DECIDED HE WAS DREAMING. BECAUSE, REALLY, THERE WAS NO other explanation for what just happened. One moment he and Carson were about to leave Shelby's café, the next she'd somehow convinced them to stay and put a quarter-full tequila bottle to good use. He didn't know why he'd agreed, but somehow he had, and now here he was, watching Shelby Harper toss her head back and take a shot.

Fuck, she was sexy. Her golden waves cascading down her shoulders, her delicate throat bobbing as she swallowed back the fiery liquid.

She made a face, then handed the bottle and shot glass to Carson, who was more than ready for the challenge. Carson swiftly took his shot and passed the bottle over.

Garrett glanced at it for a moment, debating. He had no idea what Shelby was trying to accomplish. Was she trying to get him drunk? Was she planning on jumping his bones if he did? And if so, why the hell had she asked Carson to stick around too?

Something niggled at the back of his mind, but he forced the absurd idea away.

No. *No.* Freckles or not, Shelby definitely wasn't the type who'd go for a three-way.

Was she?

"C'mon, *Johnny*," she teased after he'd hesitated too long. "Scared of a little tequila?"

Uh-oh, she'd called him Johnny. He'd once told her how he felt about the nickname. His exact words had been: "I hate it. Call me that and I'll kick your ass". But he didn't want to kick Shelby's ass at the moment, not by a long shot. She looked so damn good in that tight top, with her fair cheeks flushed from the heat and the alcohol. He wanted to kiss her. Badly. So badly he could practically taste her on his lips.

But rather than jumping across the table and capturing her mouth with his, he met her challenge and downed some alcohol instead.

The tequila burned its way down to his gut, warming his body and easing the knot of tension coiled inside him.

"God, it's so hot," Shelby said with a groan, fanning herself with one dainty hand. Then she smiled and shot to her feet. "We need ice."

Garrett admired her ass as she hurried out of the room. She was wearing a filmy blue skirt that was practically transparent, and if he looked hard enough he could see the outline of her panties. Wait. The skirt moved and...yeah, she had a thong on.

Oh Jesus.

Trying not to groan, he shifted in his chair, but no matter how he arranged himself his pants still felt exceedingly tight.

"So...I think she's trying to seduce us," Carson murmured. He looked a little startled, as if he couldn't quite believe this turn of events. "I guess I stand corrected on the freckles thing."

Garrett swallowed, not believing it either. He'd been thinking the same thing, and hearing his best friend say it confirmed his own suspicions. "She's had too much to drink," was the only reply he could come up with.

"She's not drunk, man. Walking in a straight line, not slurring her words..." Carson's mouth stretched out in a smile. "I think she knows exactly what she's doing. And exactly what she wants."

He wanted to argue, but Shelby returned with a plastic bowl filled with ice and flopped down in her chair again. When she reached for an ice cube and began trailing it down her neck, Garrett swallowed a groan.

Carson was right. Shelby knew exactly what she was doing. And her plan obviously included making her two companions as hard as granite.

A little moan slid out of her throat as she rubbed the ice along her collarbone, leaving a path of glistening moisture on her silky skin.

Garrett shifted again, but it was futile. He had a massive erection, and it only continued to grow the longer Shelby dragged that ice cube over herself. She lifted her wavy hair up and cooled the nape of her neck. Ran the ice up and down her bare arms. Brought it back to her collarbone, then—oh sweet Lord—slid her fingers under the neckline of her tank top.

It amazed him to realize that he was jealous—of the fucking ice cube. He could see her palm moving beneath her shirt, hear her sighs of contentment as she rubbed the ice over the tops of her perky tits, and all he wanted to do was push her hand away and take over.

"You guys are missing out," she teased, gesturing to the bowl on the table. "Seriously, take some ice and put it down your shirt. It feels like heaven."

Carson chuckled. "Can't speak for Garrett, but I'm having more fun watching you."

Shelby made an irritated sound and pulled her hand out of her cleavage. The ice had melted, and her fingers were wet. Garrett wanted to lean forward and lick the moisture off with his tongue. And when he finished licking her fingers, he'd tear that shirt off her body and lick everything beneath it. And then…then he'd get down on his knees, lift that skirt up to her waist and lick under there too…

Quickly averting his gaze, he clenched his fists, stunned to realize he was unbelievably close to coming. He'd almost blown his fricking load, in his pants, without so much as touching Shelby.

The woman was far more dangerous than he'd ever suspected.

"Look how nice it feels…"

He slowly uncurled his fingers and lifted his head just in time to see… yup, Shelby was running an ice cube along Carson's jaw line.

Garrett watched as she leaned in closer and traced Carson's mouth with the ice. The lucky bastard was enjoying every second of it and Garrett didn't blame him. He'd be pretty happy too if Shelby had her fingers on his mouth. Which raised the question—would he be getting a turn?

Because damn, he really, *really* wanted one. But she seemed pretty content teasing Carson to oblivion, and then she leaned even closer and...

Kissed him.

She was *kissing* his best friend.

And Garrett, fucking strangely enough, was as turned on as he was envious. He couldn't help himself, couldn't tear his eyes away from the sight of Shelby's mouth pressed against Carson's. Her tongue sliding between his friend's lips and delving into his mouth. The soft moan she gave when their tongues met.

Shockwaves of heat pulsed in Garrett's groin.

Fuck.

Fuck.

What was happening? He'd wanted this woman for an entire year, and here she was, kissing his buddy. Kissing, and running her fingers through Carson's hair, and...was he imagining it or had she just slid her other hand onto Carson's lap?

"Whoa," Carson muttered, and Garrett knew he hadn't imagined it. Shelby did indeed have her hand on his friend's crotch.

"What are you doing?" Carson asked hoarsely.

Good question.

Shelby withdrew her hand and leaned back in her chair, but Garrett saw the hint of a smile tugging at her lush lips.

"I'm going to be honest," she finally said, shifting her gaze between the two men. "I think we should go upstairs to my apartment. All three of us."

Carson's head swiveled in Garrett's direction.

Garrett kept his gaze on Shelby. "Are you serious?" he squeezed out.

"Oh yeah." She demurely clasped her hands together on her lap.

"But...why?"

Her smile transformed into a naughty grin, ocean-blue eyes sparkling with desire and amusement. "Because I want to."

Because she wanted to. It was such a simple, no-nonsense answer, and yet Garrett couldn't wrap his brain around it. Who was this wild-eyed vixen and what had she done with his sweet, freckle-faced Shelby? Shelby, the woman who baked cakes for a living, who actually cared enough to ask him how his day was, who could brighten up his world with just one small smile.

He'd spent the last year getting to know her, holding off on asking her out because he didn't want to make it seem like all he wanted to do was jump her bones. And now here she was, flat-out offering to jump *his* bones, along with the bones of his closest friend.

Part of him was troubled. Worried that he might've gotten her all wrong, that she was only looking for a good time like all the other women he'd been with.

But another part of him, the turned on part, was dying to go upstairs with her. So what if she wanted Carson to tag along? Garrett had craved this woman for so long that at this point he was willing to do anything to get her. *Take what you can get*, his body was telling him. His head, too, seemed to be in agreement, pointing out that the offer wasn't likely to stay on the table for long. A few more moments of hesitation and she'd probably kick him out and choose to go upstairs with Carson instead. Just Carson.

"Let's do it, then." The words came out before he could stop them, and once he'd thrown them out there he couldn't take them back. His legs were unusually shaky as he stood, but he managed to keep a composed front. Glancing at Carson, he added, "You up for it?"

His buddy looked surprised, shooting him a look that said, *Are you sure about this, man?*

It was actually kind of nice that Carson would request permission. Carson Scott was the type of guy who did what he wanted, when he wanted it, but when it came to his friends he was oddly considerate. Since Garrett hadn't made his feelings for Shelby a secret, it wasn't surprising that Carson would respect them.

He knew all he had to do was give an imperceptible shake of the head and Carson would hightail it outta there, but if he telepathically ordered Carson to get lost, would Shelby still want *him*? Or was a threesome a prerequisite for tonight's fantasy?

He looked over at Shelby, whose arousal was clearly written all over her flushed face, and realized the answers to either of those questions didn't matter. He was going to take what he could get. One on one, two on one, it didn't fucking matter. Not as long as he got to be with this woman.

And so he offered Carson a small nod of reassurance, because really, if a kinky ménage was what Shelby Harper had in mind, then that was exactly what he'd give her.

Chapter Three

Garrett and Carson were actually coming upstairs with her.

So they could have sex.

So the *three of them* could have sex.

She hadn't thought they'd actually agree to it. Garrett had almost fallen out of his chair when she'd suggested it. For a moment she'd even thought he'd get up and walk out the door. But whatever reluctance he might have felt had faded the second he'd stood and said *let's do it.*

Thank God for the tequila swimming around in her blood, that's for sure. She wasn't drunk by any means, but the slow burn of the alcohol and the lightness inside her head definitely made it easier to climb up the narrow staircase leading to her apartment. She didn't dare turn to look at Garrett, who was directly behind her, his breath warming the back of her neck.

She almost jumped two feet in the air when she felt his lips brush her ear. His voice was gruff as he said, "Sure you want to do this?"

They reached the door and she pushed it open, walking inside the dark living room without answering the question.

Did she want to do this? Should she back out, tell them it had been the tequila talking and that no, she had no intention of getting naked with them?

She stopped, leaned against the wall and stared at the two men who'd followed her inside, both gorgeous in their own right. Garrett, with his dark hair and rugged good looks. Carson, fair and blond with his chiseled *GQ*-model face.

She could ask them to leave, claim this was a mistake, but her body's reaction to them made it hard to open her mouth and say the words. God, what was wrong with her? Her nipples were as hard as icicles, her panties were soaked, and every cell in her body begged for the chance to be taken by these two sex gods. Two hard bodies pressed against her, two pairs of hands touching her, two mouths kissing her, two cocks—

"Shel?" Garrett prompted.

She swallowed. It was unbelievably hot in the apartment, making it hard to breathe, let alone think. Open a window, that's what she needed to do. Or turn on the fan sitting on the coffee table. But she couldn't bring herself to move. Her pussy was throbbing, her clit so painfully swollen she had to squeeze her thighs together before she keeled over.

"So how do you want to do this?" she burst out.

There, she'd finally said something. Which meant she couldn't back down now, because the *something* she'd said pretty much made it obvious she intended to do this. And jeez, did that throaty femme fatale voice actually belong to her?

"It'd help if you took off your clothes," Carson returned with a sexy chuckle.

Garrett said nothing, but his piercing brown eyes were narrowed with arousal, as well as another emotion she couldn't quite put her finger on. She wished he would come over and kiss her. She already knew what Carson's kiss tasted like. Slow, teasing, languid. Would Garrett's lips feel as soft against hers? Would he be gentle? Or would his kiss be rough, greedy?

Suddenly she couldn't wait to find out, but since they obviously expected her to get naked before they touched her, Shelby reached for the hem of her tank and pulled the thin material up and over her head. Her bra was practically pasted to her body, drops of sweat already forming between her breasts. Her fingers shook as she unhooked the front clasp and shrugged the lacy bra off her shoulders.

Neither man said a word, but their eyes widened with approval at the sight of her bare breasts. The palpable appreciation jumpstarted her confidence, and her hands were no longer trembling when she gripped the elastic waistband of her flowing skirt and took that off too. The thong came off next, and then she was naked and on display for the two sexiest guys she'd ever encountered.

Carson's soft whistle broke through the silence. "Jesus, Shelby," he hissed out. "You're fucking gorgeous."

Heat spilled over her cheeks. Both men were completely dressed, and there she was, standing in front of them without a stitch of clothing so they could openly admire her. And under their scrutiny, her nipples tightened, her breasts grew heavy and a rush of moisture pooled between her legs. Maybe it made her the slut of the century, but she couldn't wait to get started.

Evidently Garrett felt the same urgency—before she could blink he'd stepped toward her and was pulling her naked body to his clothed one. She stared at his mouth, knowing her excitement was written all over her face.

"Kiss me," she whispered.

He quickly complied by pressing his lips to hers. His mouth was hot, firm, insistent. Oh yes. Carson had kissed her like he had all the time in the world, his mouth lazy, but Garrett was more intense. His kisses were rough and hungry and passionate, as if he wanted to devour her. Well, she wanted to devour him too. So she did, sucking hard on his tongue and shamelessly rubbing against his lower body.

Breathing hard, she tugged on the bottom of his T-shirt and pulled it over his head. Underneath the shirt, his chest was all muscle, a wide expanse of hard ripples and smooth golden skin, with a dusting of light brown hair leading to the waistband of his cargo pants.

Her mouth went dry, her hand unsteady as she reached out and touched that incredible chest. She brushed her finger over a flat, brown nipple, eliciting a ragged sigh from his throat.

She was trying to decide if she was bold enough to lower her head and suck on his nipple when she felt a warm pair of hands stroking her bare back. She nearly jumped, then realized it was Carson, obviously eager to join in the fun.

Oh God, this was surreal. Her naked body sandwiched between these two big men, Carson's hands squeezing her ass, Garrett dipping his head and kissing her again. Shivers of arousal danced up and down her spine, and a resulting moan slid out of her mouth.

Garrett chuckled softly, then planted his hands on her waist and turned her around, pressing his groin into her ass as Carson filled her mouth with his tongue.

She could feel Garrett's erection nestled between her ass cheeks, and when Carson pulled her closer and parted her knees with one hard thigh she felt the ridge of his arousal too. She sighed, pushing her ass against Garrett and reaching down to rub Carson through his khakis.

"Take your pants off," she murmured.

She was addressing both of them, but Carson was the only one to reply. He offered her a lopsided grin and muttered, "Do it for me."

She found herself glancing over at Garrett, who simply stared back, his dark eyes flickering with raw heat. "Don't keep the man waiting," he said with a faint smile.

Drawing in a slow breath, she tugged at Carson's zipper. It lowered with a metallic hiss.

Shelby hesitated, unsure of what to do next. This was all so new to her, the entire experience more like a figment of her dirty imagination than a real-time occurrence.

"Help me out here," she said with a nervous laugh. "What comes next?"

Carson's blue eyes twinkled. "I do."

He took her hand and guided it inside his pants. She drew another breath, gathering every ounce of naughty courage she possessed before wrapping her fingers around his cock and stroking him.

He groaned and fumbled with his waistband, attempting to push his pants down. "Help me out here," he mimicked, his features taut with lust.

Sinking to her knees, she pulled down his khakis and boxers, wondering if the blood drumming in her ears was a result of the tequila or the hard cock that sprang up against her face. God, he was big.

She circled his tip with her index finger and he shuddered. "Shit, that's nice," he said hoarsely.

Shelby shifted her head and saw that Garrett was now leaning against the arm of her old patterned sofa. He was still clothed, still watching her with those sexy dark eyes.

She squeezed Carson's shaft, then met Garrett's gaze at the same time she took his friend's cock into her mouth.

With a moan, Carson tangled his fingers in her hair and guided her, pushing his erection deeper into her mouth. Garrett's eyes narrowed, and the fire she saw there nearly made her keel over backwards. Swallowing hard, she finally broke eye contact and focused on the task of sucking Carson's dick.

She ran her tongue along his length, flicking over the sensitive underside. He groaned in approval, still holding her against him with one hand. Her pussy throbbed as she licked him from base to tip, her body growing hotter and tighter the longer she moved her mouth up and down his cock. The room was quiet save for Carson's ragged breathing and the suction sounds of her mouth over his dick.

"Bedroom," came Garrett's rough voice.

She tore her lips away from Carson's cock, realizing for the first time that they hadn't even made it to a bed yet. She was on her knees in the middle of her living room, Carson's erection hovering in front of her face while Garrett watched from the couch. The scene was so deliciously dirty that she sagged forward, the carpet scratching her bare knees. He was right. They definitely needed a bed.

Shelby couldn't remember getting up, couldn't recall how Carson ended up lying on her bed while she kneeled between his legs and continued driving him wild with her tongue, but somehow they got there, and suddenly Garrett's hands were stroking her from behind. The mattress dipped, the springs creaked, and she gasped when she felt his fingers tugging on her nipples.

Was it possible to be this turned on? There were too many things going on at once. Carson's cock in her mouth, Garrett's palms on her breasts, his erection pressing against her ass.

Garrett's hot breath fanned across the nape of her neck. "You want me to fuck you while you suck Carson's dick?" he muttered, rolling her nipples between his fingers.

All she could do was whimper.

He tipped her forward and she gasped when he slid one finger into her already sopping-wet pussy. "You love this, don't you, Shelby?" he taunted, then pressed his lips to her neck.

Pleasure surged through her. She felt like a volcano that had been dormant for decades, only to erupt out of the blue and cover everything, everyone, with hot smoldering lava and to hell with the consequences. She pushed her butt into Garrett's exploring finger, her lips still wrapped around Carson's shaft.

A delighted cry tore out of her throat when Garrett worked another finger into her pussy. He slid those two long fingers in and out of her, so hard and deep that she almost bit down on Carson, who obviously sensed her inability to multitask and gently pulled her up.

She found herself sprawled over Carson's rippled chest, her breasts pressed against his defined pecs, while her ass jutted out to accommodate Garrett's talented fingers.

Carson pinched her nipples, rolling the rigid peaks with his fingers. He smiled when she let out a soft sigh, then tugged on her hair and angled her head so they were at eye-level, so he could brush his lips over hers. His tongue slid into her mouth, dueling with hers, stealing the breath right out of her lungs. Her body was overcome with sensation—Garrett's fingers inside her, Carson's hands squeezing and playing with her breasts, the hot tongue inside her mouth and the cock twitching against her belly.

"Do you like having John finger you while my tongue is in your mouth?" Carson whispered against her lips.

"Yes," she squeezed out.

"I'm going crazy here," he added, his features creased with pure hunger. He grasped one of her hands and dragged it down to his heavy cock, urging her to jerk him off.

Garrett's husky voice drifted from behind. "Will you come if I keep doing this, baby?" He added a third finger into the mix, then began stroking her clit with his thumb.

"Eventually," she managed to utter, her mind spinning from the tornado of pleasure assaulting her body.

"Eventually?" Garrett made a tsking sound. "Can't have that. We want you to come now, don't we, Carson?"

"Oh yeah."

Garrett pulled his fingers out and she almost wept with disappointment. A second later she was weeping with joy, because she was on her back and Garrett's head was between her legs. His warm mouth covered her pussy, his tongue flicked over her clit and…oh yes…his fingers were back too. The pleasure was so intense she could barely keep her eyes open, let alone stroke Carson, who'd shifted and was now lying next to her. He didn't seem to mind that her hand had stopped moving. Instead, he just pushed that hand away and lowered his mouth to her breast.

"Come on, Shelby," Carson murmured. "I want to see you lose control."

Within moments he got his wish, because it was pretty darn hard *not* to lose control when these two men were driving her mad with their tongues. With Carson sucking on her aching nipples and Garrett licking the hell out of her, Shelby exploded. The orgasm seized her body in a rush of blinding pleasure that had her crying out. The room spun, the mattress sagged, the air became too thick to breathe.

She whimpered, trying to wiggle away from Garrett's unwavering tongue, but he gripped her hips with his hands and kept her in place. Continued to finger her and suck on her clit until the world tilted again and a surprising second orgasm tore through her.

Oh God.

When the waves of release finally ebbed, she could barely move. She heard Carson's soft chuckle against her breasts, Garrett's ragged breaths against her pussy, and wondered if it was supposed to feel this good. Why hadn't anyone ever told her how good it would feel to have two men make her come?

"You okay?" Garrett asked with a touch of humor in his voice. He lifted his head from her thighs and sat up, lightly stroking her stomach.

"I'm...great." She blinked herself out of her orgasmic trance, noticing that he still had his cargo pants on. "Take those off already," she complained.

Without addressing her grievance, he pulled a condom out of one of the many pockets lining his pants. Flicking the square packet at his friend, Garrett said, "I've only got one."

A tiny pretzel of disappointment knotted in her belly. As appealing as she found Carson, he wouldn't have been her first choice as the winner of the one-condom raffle. But she didn't voice her frustration, not wanting to shatter any macho egos here.

Carson easily caught the condom that had been thrown to him and then uttered words that had her disappointment dissolving into delight. "There's a couple in my wallet. Think my pants are somewhere in the living room." He grinned at Shelby as if to remind her she'd been the one to dispose of those pants.

"I'll grab 'em," Garrett said, then disappeared out the door.

Shelby stared after him, admiring the way his pants hugged his sexy ass. The moment of admiration was brief, though, because the next thing she knew Carson was covering her body with his.

He kissed her, and gone were those lazy kisses he'd been giving her when Garrett was sucking on her clit. Carson's tongue filled her mouth and then he drove his cock into her without warning.

That first thrust stole her breath. A small moan found its way out of her mouth, reverberating against Carson's greedy tongue.

"Fuck, Shelby, you're so tight."

His rough, erratic pace drove her wild. She arched her hips to take him in deeper. God, this felt fantastic. Was it wrong that it was this damn fantastic? She'd been lusting after Garrett for so long that the way her body responded to Carson almost felt like a betrayal.

But Garrett didn't seem betrayed as he walked back into the bedroom. He paused in the doorway for a second, watching as Carson fucked her, and then finally, *finally*, he started to unbutton his pants.

Shelby tore her mouth away from Carson's and watched as Garrett approached the bed, pulling down his zipper as he walked. She couldn't unglue her gaze from him, mesmerized by each small movement. His hands pushing his pants down. His fingers on the waistband of his black boxer briefs.

Watching her watch him, he slowly removed the boxers, smiling faintly when her eyes widened. His cock jutted out, long and thick and rock hard.

"Like what you see?" Garrett asked gruffly.

She managed a nod, her mouth too dry for her to speak. Then she moaned, because Carson had slowed his pace and was teasing her body with deep, leisurely thrusts the way the sight of Garrett's erection teased her eyes.

Garrett moved closer, his dark eyes so unbelievably intense that Shelby felt the first swells of orgasm flutter to the surface. She sucked in a breath, her inner muscles clamping over Carson's cock. She was seconds away from losing control again, and Garrett obviously knew it because in the blink of an eye he was on the bed, kneeling in front of her and parting her lips with his erection. His tip slid into her mouth and the taste of him was all it took.

Shelby came again.

"Jesus," Carson groaned. "Keep squeezing my cock like that…yeah, Shel…just like that."

She couldn't seem to stop moaning, the sounds muffled against Garrett's dick. As shockwaves of pleasure rocketed through her body, she lapped at him with her tongue, his husky groans only heightening each wave of her orgasm.

"Fuck, I'm going to come," Carson hissed, his fingers curling tightly over her hips.

She opened her eyes in time to see his features grow taut, his eyes glaze over with sheer bliss. Carson pushed into her, once, twice, his thrusts jerky, and then he exploded too.

When she felt him shudder from the climax, she had to pull her mouth away from Garrett's cock in order to smile. Carson had doubted her sexual abilities when he'd called her vanilla, and she wanted to shout from the rooftops that the freckle-faced good girl had just made Doubting Carson come. And come hard. The ragged breaths rolling out of his chest were enough to widen her smile into a full-blown grin.

"You okay?" she teased, tracing his strong jaw with her fingers.

He stared down at her with heavy-lidded eyes. "Oh yeah. That was amazing."

She was still smiling as Carson slowly withdrew and stumbled off the bed. He rolled the condom off with one hand and shot her an unbelievably satisfied look before ambling into the bathroom.

And then she was alone with Garrett. Whose cock was still inches from her mouth. Whose eyes were still glimmering with raw hunger.

She arched one brow at him before leaning closer and flicking her tongue against his cock. He groaned when she sucked the drop of pre-come from his tip. Tangled his fingers in her hair and tried to pull her even closer.

She quickly leaned back, enjoying the disappointment she saw flashing in his dark eyes.

"So Carson gets to have all the fun?" he grumbled.

She responded with a soft laugh. "Actually, Carson was just my warm-up." Again, that throaty voice slipped out of her mouth as if it belonged to her. "Now I'm *really* getting started."

"Oh really?"

"Yep."

With another laugh, Shelby sat up and climbed onto his lap, pressing her palms on his extraordinary chest and forcing him to lean back against the headboard. Then she twined her arms around his neck and kissed him.

Chapter Four

OH CHRIST. GARRETT DIDN'T THINK HE COULD EVER GET ENOUGH OF Shelby's sexy lips. She kissed like a fucking dream, her mouth pliant and warm, her tongue slick and eager. If he died right now, with Shelby's curvy naked body in his lap and her tongue in his mouth, then he'd die an unbelievably happy man.

"I love your lips," she whispered, surprising him by voicing the same thought he'd been having.

She pulled back and dragged her index finger over his bottom lip, her touch gentle. She was looking at him like he was a juicy Thanksgiving turkey she couldn't wait to dig her teeth into. Blue eyes glimmering with heat. Cheeks flushed with arousal.

His gaze slid south, and sure enough, her nipples had pebbled into two tight peaks. Had she been this turned on for Carson? It was ridiculous that he would be thinking about that now, making jealous comparisons, but he couldn't help it.

Shelby was so different from the women he'd shared with Carson. She might've surprised the hell out of him by suggesting a threesome, but Garrett was certain she didn't do things like that often. It was obvious she was enjoying herself—she'd already come three times, for fuck's sake—but there was no doubt in his mind that she was enjoying this part of the night a lot more. Him and her. One on one. Kissing the way he'd wanted them to kiss for more than a year now.

"And your tongue," she added breathlessly. "I love your tongue even more than your lips."

He chuckled and swept his hands over her tailbone. Her skin was damp with sweat, and he was about to offer to turn on the ceiling fan when a phone rang. At first Garrett thought it was his, but his pants were sitting at the foot of the bed, and the ringing sounded like it was coming from the living room.

"Shit," Carson said as he came out of the bathroom. "That's me."

Carson was still as naked as the day he was born, but Garrett wasn't fazed. He'd seen Carson naked dozens of times. The sight of his friend's cock and bare ass no longer made him uncomfortable.

Carson hurried out of the bedroom, his footsteps echoing in the hallway. A moment later, his muffled voice sounded from the living room.

Garrett turned to find Shelby staring at him, her expression one of curiosity. "You guys do this, um, threesome thing often, don't you?" she said awkwardly.

He shrugged. "We were a lot wilder a few years back, before we finished BUD/S training. We don't do this kinda thing too much anymore."

She looked surprised. "Really?"

He offered a *what-can-you-do?* smile. "People grow up. Besides, we're out of the country a lot, which makes it hard to, you know, get shitfaced and do the whole ménage thing."

"So…why tonight then?"

Deciding that honesty was probably the best policy, he raised his hand to her cheek and stroked her skin. "I wanted to be with you. And you wanted a threesome, so…" He let his voice drift.

She was quiet for so long he was surprised when she spoke again. "I wanted to be with you too, John." She averted her eyes. "I would've wanted it even if Carson weren't here."

Before he could respond to that confession, the sound of footsteps interrupted him.

Carson reappeared in the doorway, a frazzled expression on his face. "Jenny's car broke down." He had his pants on, but they were unbuttoned and he zipped them up while bending down to retrieve his shirt from the floor. "My sister," he explained when he caught Shelby's questioning expression.

"Is she all right?" Garrett asked. He wasn't surprised, though, since Jenny made it a habit of calling her big brother whenever she needed to get out of a jam. Which was often. Trouble seemed to follow that girl around like a stray dog.

"Car overheated," Carson replied. He poked his head through the neck hole of his shirt. "She claims she'll die of hyperthermia if I don't come and help." He rolled his eyes, adding, "I, personally, think she doesn't have enough money to pay for a tow truck. She blew her last paycheck on a pair of six hundred dollar shoes—who the fuck pays that much money for shoes?"

Carson walked over to the edge of the bed, where a very naked Shelby was still straddling Garrett's lap. With a faint grin, Carson dipped his head and planted a light peck on Shelby's forehead. Garrett immediately experienced another flicker of jealousy, but he smothered the irritating emotion.

"I just want to say that you, Shelby, were absolutely incredible. I'd also like to say we'll do this again sometime, but I highly doubt Garrett will agree to share next time." Carson laughed. "He likes your freckles too much. Not so much your fancy coffees, but he totally digs the freckles." He moved away from the bed. "I'll see myself out."

With a mock salute, Carson left the room. A moment later, the sound of the front door latching echoed throughout the apartment.

And there Garrett was. Alone with Shelby. Naked with Shelby. Just like he'd always dreamed.

He shifted his gaze back to her gorgeous face, wanting to kiss her again, but her perplexed expression made him reconsider.

"What did he mean about you not liking my coffee?" she asked slowly.

Garrett managed a noncommittal shrug. "Nothing. Carson rarely makes any sense." He tried to stroke one of her amazing tits, but she swatted his hand away.

Then she crossed her arms over her breasts, as if covering herself up would force him to have this conversation. He almost laughed. She had no idea how distracting her body was, covered up or not.

"You don't like my mocha lattes," she accused, her eyes widening with horror.

Garrett sighed.

"But…you buy one practically every day you're not at the base or off on assignment. You've probably spent hundreds of dollars buying coffee from me. And the cakes—" She gasped. "Do you even like cake?"

He couldn't help but smile. "Yes, Shelby, I like cake. And yes, I might prefer good old black coffee to the fancy shit you sell, but…"

"But what?" Her voice was soft.

"But I'd drink antifreeze if it gave me a chance to see you, all right?"

Something dawned in her dazzling blue eyes. "You come in just to see me?"

"Afraid so."

"Because we're...friends?"

He sighed again. "That too. But mainly because I have a huge fucking thing for you and I've been trying to figure out how to tell you for about a year now."

His confession had obviously stunned her, because she just sat there, staring at him, her firm thighs cradling his still-hard dick. The silence dragged on for so long he wondered if he should repeat the words, maybe in a different language this time since she honestly didn't seem to comprehend what he'd said.

She spoke before he could. "You have a thing for me? Even though you think I'm vanilla?"

He blinked. "What? Who said—" He cursed suddenly. "Shit, I knew you were listening in the doorway when I was talking to Carson." He studied her face, suddenly wondering if...had she actually...? "Did you bring us up here to prove something to me?"

She didn't answer, but the telltale blush on her cheeks said it all.

"Jesus, Shelby!"

Frowning at his harsh tone, she crossed her arms tighter over her chest. "It wasn't the only reason. I really did want...I've always...it was a fantasy of mine, okay?" She looked defensive as she said it. "Maybe it makes me a huge slut in your eyes, but I've always wanted to experience... you know, two guys."

Now she just looked embarrassed. She tried to climb off his lap, but Garrett gripped her waist and rolled them both over so that she was lying on her back and he was propped up on his elbow, looming over her. Again she attempted to wiggle away from him, so he simply quieted her with a long kiss. She gave a sharp intake of breath before kissing him back.

"I'm not judging you," he murmured when he pulled his mouth away. "And I don't think you're a slut, not at all. I just don't want you to think that you need to, you know, screw my friend in order to make yourself more appealing in my eyes. Truth is, you've always been pretty damn appealing to me."

"Then why didn't you ever say something?" Her eyes were soft as she reached up and touched his chin. "I've been flirting with you for a year, Garrett. You could've given me a sign that you were interested."

She'd been flirting with him for a year? Jeez. Maybe if he hadn't spent so much time trying to figure out a way to ask her out, he would've picked up on that flirting. As it was, he felt like a complete idiot for missing the signals she'd apparently been sending his way.

"I didn't want you to think I only wanted sex from you," he admitted.

"So all that stuff about my freckles and me not being into kinky sex…?"

"That was Carson trying to convince me you weren't interested in me because of my reputation for being a, uh…"

"Man-ho?" she supplied.

He leaned down and kissed the mischievous smile right off her lips. "My man-ho days are over. I was serious when I said I want to be with you."

"This, coming from the guy who just watched his best friend have sex with me."

"I'll admit, that made me jealous as hell," he said gruffly, tucking a strand of blonde hair behind her ear. "But I thought…well, like you said, it was a fantasy of yours. And now that you've gotten it out of your system, maybe we could focus on *my* fantasy."

Her eyes twinkled. "And what would that be?"

"You."

He brushed his lips over hers, and this time when she deepened the kiss he didn't pull back. No more talking. Right now all he wanted to do was lose himself in Shelby's soft body and sweet lips. He licked his way from her mouth to her neck, sucking gently on her skin and inhaling the intoxicating scent of her. She smelled like flowers and lavender and, ironically, vanilla. But Carson had been dead wrong earlier, because there was nothing vanilla about Shelby. No other woman had ever managed to turn him on this fiercely.

He moved his mouth from her neck down to her breasts, drawing one nipple between his lips. He flicked his tongue over the pebbled nub, enjoying the way she moaned and tangled her fingers in his hair to bring him deeper. He suckled on her other nipple and got another moan for his effort, and then Shelby's fingers left his hair and were stroking his cock until he could barely see straight.

"You'll make me come if you keep doing that," he growled.

"I thought man-hoes had excellent restraint."

"I meant what I said about those days being over. I haven't been with anyone for more than a year, Shel."

Her hand dropped from his dick, her expression both startled and wary. "Seriously?"

"Seriously," he confirmed.

The look in her eyes told him she wasn't sure whether to believe him, and again he decided to put an end to all the talking. They could discuss it later—right now he just wanted to enjoy being naked with Shelby.

The heat in the bedroom was overwhelming, both from the heat wave outside and the sparks sizzling between them. Inhaling some much-needed oxygen, Garrett slid his hand between her legs and touched her clit, then lower, groaning when he found her pussy soaking wet.

"Damn it," he choked out.

"What's the matter?" He could hear the smile in her voice.

"I planned on going slow."

"And you're speaking in the past tense because…?"

"Because the plan was shot to hell the second I felt *this*." He palmed her, then pushed two fingers inside all that wetness. "Fuck, I need to be inside you."

He grabbed the condom lying next to them and rolled it onto his dick. A second later he was on top of her, driving into her sweet heat to the hilt.

"Johnny," she gasped, so much pleasure loaded into her voice he didn't bother reminding her how much he hated being called that. Truth was, the name sounded hot coming from Shelby's lips.

He slid his hands underneath her and cupped her firm ass, pushing himself in deeper, buried so far inside her pussy he thought he might be hurting her. But her soft moans and the way she tilted her hips spoke otherwise, and soon he was pumping into her without an ounce of finesse. He felt like a horny teenager again, needing to drive his cock into her over and over again, needing to explode in a climax that was one year in the making.

Shelby didn't seem to mind. If anything, she was moving more erratically than he was, meeting him thrust for thrust, begging him to go faster, and, when fast didn't seem to be enough for her, harder.

"John...I'm going to...oh God..." She dug her fingers into his back, which was now soaked with sweat, and proceeded to fall apart beneath him.

The look of ecstasy in her eyes as she came was enough to send him flying over that same cliff. White-hot pleasure shot down his spine and grabbed hold of his balls, and then he was coming too, his heart damn near bursting, his eyes blinded by the light exploding in front of them.

"Jesus." He gasped out a breath, trying to put what he'd just experienced into more eloquent words. "That was...Jesus."

Shelby wasn't capable of talking any more than he was, because she simply gave a contented sigh and wrapped her arms tighter around him.

He knew he must be crushing her, so he gently tried rolling off, but she held him in place and murmured, "Stay."

Smiling, he slowly withdrew his still-hard cock from her tightness, never moving off her while he took off the condom. Then he planted a soft kiss on her lips and said, "Don't worry, I don't plan on going anywhere."

Chapter Five

SHELBY WOKE UP THE NEXT MORNING TO THE SOUND OF RAIN POUNDING against the bedroom window. She and Garrett hadn't bothered shutting the curtains last night, and she turned her head and watched as fat raindrops streaked down the glass. Looked like the heat wave had finally broken.

The heat level between the sheets, however, was still at record-breaking levels.

"Don't you ever stop to rest?" she asked as Garrett slid one warm hand underneath her panties and teased her clit with his fingers.

"Nope." He snuggled closer to her, looking ridiculously adorable with his dark hair tousled from sleep and his brown eyes twinkling with mischief.

She still couldn't believe he'd stayed the entire night. She'd been expecting him to freak out or something, decide he'd made a mistake by sleeping with her and jump out of bed in horror. She thought she'd wake up to find his side of the bed empty, the imprint of his body the only sign that he'd actually been there.

But here he was. Playful and awake and not in the least bit remorseful about what they'd done. It was obvious the only remorse he felt was over the fact that she was still wearing panties, but he quickly took care of that.

"We should really get up," she said reluctantly as his fingers continued their exploration.

He grabbed her hand and dragged it to his groin. "I'm already up."

A jolt of desire shook her body when she felt his hard-on. Oh yeah. He was definitely up.

She curled her fingers over his shaft and slowly began to stroke him, all the while wondering what had come over her. The alarm clock on her nightstand read nine a.m. She had an entire refrigerator of cakes that needed to be delivered, and yet she couldn't stop touching Garrett, couldn't dissuade her body from responding to those talented fingers and the way his thumb circled her clit and... Screw the cakes. Who needed so much sugar this early anyway?

She kicked the tangle of bedcovers off her legs and climbed onto his lap. "Fine. You talked me into it."

Laughing, he reached up and cupped her chin. His warm hands pulled her face toward his. A second later his lips covered hers. The kiss was gentle, a flick of tongue, a nip of teeth, and then he moved his mouth to her neck and lightly sucked on her skin.

Heat curled inside her, then spread through her body, leaving sizzling shivers in its wake. Garrett's morning stubble chafed her skin, but the small abrasions only turned her on more. She loved his rough masculinity.

"I don't know how I went a whole year without touching you," he groaned into her neck, wrapping his arms tightly around her waist.

She inhaled the spicy scent of him, threaded her fingers through his hair and forced his mouth back to hers. This time his kiss was loaded with hunger, and she responded eagerly, pushing her tongue into his mouth and savoring the taste of him. She'd never experienced kisses like this before, hot and hurried and so damn erotic that even her tongue began to tingle.

Leaving one hand on her hips, he moved the other around and lowered it between her legs. Without breaking the kiss, he stroked her deftly, massaged her clit, and then pushed a finger inside her, until the dull ache of desire filled her veins and her thighs trembled.

"No, not yet," she breathed, trying to push his hand away. "I want you inside me."

She reached for the nightstand, where a lone condom sat, just waiting to be torn open. She was suddenly grateful she hadn't let Garrett use it when he'd woken her up with a kiss in the middle of the night. Carson had only had two condoms in his wallet, and since she'd wanted to conserve them she'd rewarded Garrett's wake-up kiss with a blowjob that would go down in history—no pun intended—and now she was glad she'd had the foresight to be condom-stingy.

"You're a sex maniac," Garrett teased as she ripped the corner of the packet and practically threw the condom at him.

"Look at who I've got in my bed. I waited a year for you too, you know."

He rolled the latex over his impressive hard-on, tilting his head as he said, "I still can't believe I missed all those signals you were sending." His hand moved back between her thighs and he groaned when he felt how wet she was. "We could've been doing this ages ago."

She straddled him again and guided his cock where she wanted it. "Sure, but don't you think it was worth the wait?"

He thrust upwards. "Oh yeah."

God, she didn't think she'd ever get used to having him buried inside her. It felt so good, so *right.*

She whimpered when he withdrew, wiggling around in an attempt to bring him back where he belonged, but he wouldn't let her. Chuckling softly, he flipped her onto her back and took control, teasing her opening with the tip of his cock.

"I told you I want you inside," she complained.

"Yeah, well, I want it to last. I want you so bad I'm about to explode."

"Then explode."

He shot her a rogue grin. "Not until you do."

She gave one final attempt at getting her way, but he grasped her wrist before she could reach for his dick. Then he took her other wrist, shoved both up over her head and locked them together with one strong hand.

"Be patient," he ordered, his dark eyes flickering with both arousal and amusement.

"Yes sir."

Very slowly, he rubbed his cock over her opening again, dragging it up and down her wet slit. Each time his tip brushed her clit she shuddered. And each time she arched her hips he withdrew and shook his head with disapproval. He was still restraining her hands, but his hard grip only drove her wild. She kinda liked being at his mercy, lying beneath him while he did whatever he wanted to her feverish body.

Her breasts started to tingle, her nipples hardened, her pussy clenched, and yet he still didn't enter her. His torturous teasing became too much. Her body was too primed, and when he finally plunged into her, there was no stopping the orgasm.

It hit her like a freight train. Rushed through her blood, clamped onto her muscles and sucked all the breath right out of her lungs. She heard herself moaning, but the sound was muffled by the roar of her pulse in her ears.

Garrett didn't slow down, didn't let her recover. He just tightened his hold on her wrists, biting down on her neck and filling the room with husky groans that signaled he was close.

She wrapped her legs around his waist, her bare feet resting on his taut backside as she lifted her hips off the mattress to bring him in deeper. Keeping her eyes open, she watched as his features strained and his eyes grew heavy-lidded.

"Come on, Johnny," she murmured, loving the expression on his face, loving that she was the one who put it there.

He buried his face in the curve of her neck, his cock began to pulsate, and then—*oh yes*—he was coming inside her. She could feel his heart racing, thudding against her breasts like an erratic tribal drum. He groaned, thrust one last time, then grew slack.

"Jesus," he wheezed out. "Is it just me or does it only get better with us?"

Finally letting go of her wrists, he rolled over and pulled her on top of him. She pressed her face against his chest and hooked one leg over his muscular thighs. They lay there for a few long moments, neither of them speaking, neither of them moving, until Garrett reached down and laced his fingers through hers.

"It was definitely worth the wait," he murmured, answering her earlier question.

Her heart leaped up and did a little flip. God, she was outrageously into this man. She'd never imagined he could be so tender, so sweet. She wished she could lie in bed with him forever, hold his hand and kiss him and wake up to his sexy face every morning for the rest of her life.

"Let's stay here forever," he mumbled, echoing her thoughts.

She stroked his rippled chest and planted a kiss on one flat nipple. "I'd love to." The image of a refrigerator full of cakes floated into the foreground of her brain. "But I can't," she added reluctantly.

She shifted and his fingers instantly curled over her hip. "No getting up."

A sigh slid out of her throat. "I have to."

"I forbid it."

Laughing, she disentangled herself from his embrace and got to her feet. Her legs almost gave out on her, the sweet aftershocks of her orgasm still fluttering through her body. "I'm serious. I have an entire fridge full of cakes that need to be delivered." The alarm clock now read ten-thirty. Damn. She was already cutting it close. A lot of the cakes needed to be delivered by noon.

"Can't you do the deliveries later?" Garrett grumbled.

She smiled at the disappointment in his eyes. "I really can't. But if you want, you can be my driver and hang out with me all day."

No sooner were the words out of her mouth than Garrett's cell phone went off. He swore softly, leaning over the side of the bed and reaching for his cargo pants. He fished his cell out, frowned when he saw the number on the screen, and lifted the phone to his ear. "Garrett," he said briskly.

Shelby watched as he listened to whatever was being said on the other end of the line. He didn't say much, except a couple "Yessirs", and a quick, "I'll be right there". Then he hung up, and the disappointment in his eyes deepened into regret.

"That was my commander," he told her.

"Oh." She swallowed. "I take it you have to go?"

He nodded.

"Overseas?"

He was already out of bed and fumbling for his clothes. "Probably."

She swallowed harder. "How long will you be gone?"

"No idea, babe. It could be hours, days, weeks, months…" Voice trailing, he pulled on his pants and zipped them up, put on his shirt and headed for the bathroom.

She heard him turn on the faucet, then flush the toilet. He was gone only for a moment, but a moment was all it took for old memories to make a tired attack. She couldn't remember how many times she'd woken up in the morning—or n the middle of the night—to the sound of Matthew's phone ringing. How many times she'd bid him goodbye, only to spend weeks worrying that he'd get shot in the jungle or get blown up by a land mine. Not that she'd had to worry. Oh no. Matt had been in constant danger, sure, but it turned out most of the danger came from the prostitutes and random strangers he hooked up with in whatever foreign country he'd been deployed to.

Question was, did Garrett share the same habits?

It was an unwelcome thought, not to mention a silly one. Raking both hands through her hair, she leaned against the bedroom door for support, wishing she could exorcise the insecurities out of her brain, out of her heart. She had no right to worry about what Garrett might or might not do when he was away. She wasn't his girlfriend. Besides, seeing as she'd had sex with one of his closest friends last night, she really wasn't in a position to judge or reprimand.

"I'm a SEAL, Shel." Garrett's quiet voice filled the room, and when she lifted her head she saw him standing in the bathroom doorway, obviously aware of the distress in her eyes. "When the team gets called, we've got no choice but to go wherever they send us."

"I know." Shoot. Did he notice the wobble in her voice?

Yep, he noticed. His expression softened as he stepped toward her and pulled her into his arms. His body was solid and warm against hers, his lips soft as he kissed her on the forehead. "I'll be back before you know it. And then we can continue what we started last night, okay?"

"Um. And will you be starting a similar, um, enterprise with someone else? You know, if you meet a woman when you're gone?"

The words came out before she could stop them, and from the flash of hurt she saw in his eyes, she knew she should've worked harder to rein in her fear and insecurity.

Garrett's hands dropped from her waist. "I can't believe you asked me that." He turned away from her, heading to the bed where he'd left his cell. He tucked the phone into his pocket. "You honestly think that low of me?"

Uh-oh.

When he turned back, the hurt on his face had tripled, his features now creased with disbelief and anger.

"I…" She tried to find the right thing to say, if there even was one. "The guy I dated before…he used to fuck around whenever he was away, okay?"

"No, not okay." A muscle twitched in his handsome jaw. "I'm *nothing* like Matthew—yeah, I know all about Matthew, your Marine, and yeah, I heard rumors that he couldn't keep his dick in his pants. But I don't do shit like that. I don't screw around on women I happen to care about."

"Garrett…" The fire in his eyes made her reconsider. Closing her mouth, she simply sighed and waited for him to get it all out.

"You think I'd say everything I said, about wanting you, about how crazy I am about you, and then turn around and fuck a stranger? Never mind that I'll be on the job, most likely in a remote corner of the world where the only women I'll encounter would rather strap bombs to their chests than fuck Americans, but damn it. You think I'd do that to you?"

She drew a long breath, suddenly feeling ridiculous for comparing this man to her ex. Garrett might have a wild past, but she believed him when he claimed to have been celibate for the last year. And in that year, he'd shown up at the café almost daily, buying lattes he didn't even like just so he could see her. And last night…God, last night he'd actually watched her have sex with his best friend just because he wanted to let her have the fantasy, because he wanted to be with her. And the way he kissed her…it was packed with way more emotion than anything she'd ever experienced.

Damn it, she really was an idiot.

Garrett must've agreed, because he was already making a swift move for the door. "Fuck this," he muttered. "Obviously our friendship this past year taught you nothing about me. Obviously everything that happened last night—and just minutes ago—didn't make any impact on you either. If you don't want to trust me, fine, don't trust me. Screw you, Shelby. I won't jump through hoops over something some other jerk did."

"Garrett—" But it was too late. He was already gone, and jeez, but the man could move. She'd barely made it two steps out of the bedroom after him when she heard the door of the apartment slam shut.

A few moments later, the distant sound of an engine starting filled her ears, and then there was nothing but the pounding of the rain against the windows.

Chapter Six

GARRETT WAS HEADING ACROSS THE BASE TOWARD THE WAITING helicopter when a familiar voice stopped him in his tracks.

He froze for a second, then turned around and sure enough, Shelby was hurrying toward him. She wore a pair of faded jeans and a bright green T-shirt, and her wavy blonde hair was pretty much soaked from the rain.

He managed to hide his surprise as she walked toward him with quick strides. What was she doing here? After the way he'd left things at her apartment, he hadn't expected to see her again this soon. If ever.

Damn, he'd really fucked up, blowing up at her like that, but could anyone really blame him? He'd made it obvious how much he liked her, how badly he wanted to be with her, and in return she'd asked him if he was going to screw someone else when he was gone. Her distrust in him had been crushing. Maybe he shouldn't have yelled at her the way he had, but hell, how could she have so little faith in him?

"Do you have a minute?" she asked, pushing wet strands of hair out of her eyes.

It was possibly the most absurd question she could've asked. Not only was the sound of the helicopter blades whirring a clear sign that no, he didn't have a minute, but her polite tone made him want to kick something.

"Who let you out here?" he returned. His question made more sense, anyway, considering civilians weren't usually allowed in this part of the base. Plus, the visitors' badge clipped to her waistband was the kind usually designated for team wives or girlfriends. How the hell had she gotten one of those?

"I did," came another voice.

Garrett glanced past Shelby's delicate shoulders and saw Carson striding toward them.

"Got her the badge, too," Carson said, giving Garrett a quick wink. Then, stopping only to give Shelby a quick side hug, he slung his duffel bag over his shoulder and headed for the helicopter, where the rest of the team was waiting.

"Don't fuck this up," Carson called without turning around, his words muffled by the rotors.

Garrett glanced back at Shelby. "So…what's up?" Wonderful. Another stupid question to join the mix.

"I couldn't let you leave without…"

She hesitated, and his brain quickly filled in the blanks.

Breaking up with you.

Voicing my extreme dislike of you.

Kissing you.

"Apologizing," she finished.

"Apologizing," he repeated.

"Yeah." A shaky breath slipped out of her mouth. "I acted like an idiot. A jealous, insecure idiot. And you had every right to walk out on me the way you did."

He shook his head. "I should've stayed."

"Well, I shouldn't have asked you if you planned on sleeping with someone else when you're gone. And I definitely shouldn't have compared you to my ex."

"I shouldn't have said 'screw you'."

She laughed. "That was kind of harsh, but I think I deserved it." Her laughter faded quickly, and he could see the uncertainty floating in her gorgeous blue eyes. "Can you forgive me, Garrett?"

Jesus, he couldn't remember the last time a woman had stood before him and asked for his forgiveness. Usually he was the one doing the asking.

"I know you're probably still mad," she continued, "but I really am sorry for the stuff I said, and I really do want to be with you when you get back. Whenever that is. I don't care if it's a day or a week or a month. I'll wait. I promise to be here when you come home."

Her words were so earnest that his heart expanded. His mouth went dry, and he couldn't get any words out, which wasn't a good thing, because Shelby's face fell as she took his silence for rejection.

"Yeah, that was probably dumb," she said with a self-deprecating smile. "The *I'll wait for you* part. A little too rom-com, huh?" Her gaze drifted to the helicopter roaring behind them. "You should go. I'll just get out of your way and—"

He kissed her. Just kissed her, right there in front of a chopper full of SEALs, most of whom started whistling.

"It wasn't dumb," he murmured into her lips. "And I'm not mad, Shel. I was before, but God knows I can never stay mad at you." A drop of rain fell directly on her freckled nose and he leaned down to kiss it away. "I'm not going to screw around on you like your asshole boyfriend did, and now that I know you'll be waiting here for me when I get back, I'll work my ass off to make sure I come home as fast as I can, okay?"

Shelby beamed at him. "Is that a promise?"

"It's a guarantee."

"Good." She leaned up on her tiptoes and brushed her lips over his, then gently pushed him away. "You should go."

"I really should." Yet he couldn't stop himself from kissing her once more. This time he slipped her a little tongue.

"Go," she ordered, looking breathless and happy and so ridiculously hot he was almost tempted to face his CO's wrath by being a smartass and asking if he could take the next chopper. But Shelby gave him another shove. "Go."

"Fine," he grumbled.

"I'll see you when you get back."

"Good."

He'd only taken a few steps when he stopped and turned to shoot her a devilish look. "Hey, you know that ice thing you were doing last night?" he called. "When you were rubbing it all over yourself and pretty much driving me crazy?"

Laughing, she raised a brow and waited for him to continue.

"Well, when I come home, we're taking out the ice again. I don't care if there's a heat wave or not. I'm definitely rubbing a couple of ice cubes all over your very un-vanilla self, all right?"

"Is that a promise?" she called back.

"Nope." He grinned and repeated his earlier words. "It's a guarantee."

The End

Up next: Carson's story! Keep reading for Heat of Passion...

Heat of Passion

An Out of Uniform Novella

Elle Kennedy

Prologue

As far as bachelor parties went, this one fucking sucked. Normally it was the best man's job to organize the stag, and Carson Scott had been tossing around wild and kinky ideas in his head ever since his best friend got engaged. But had any of those wild and kinky ideas seen the light of day? Nope. Because Garrett and Shelby wanted to plan it themselves—and make it a joint shindig.

Spending time with Shelby's hot friends might've been fun, except they were all married, engaged or attached. *All* of them. And since almost every guy on Garrett's SEAL team, including Carson, was single, the chances of hooking up with a female member of the bridal party were zero.

Fortunately, the bachelor/bachelorette party was being held at the Hot Zone, the newest nightclub in San Diego, so the chances of hooking up with a non-wedding-related chick were looking pretty good.

Carson lifted his beer to his lips and stepped closer to the second-floor railing that overlooked the crowded dance floor below. Hot Zone was one of those establishments that didn't care much for lighting. Darkness fell over the entire club, broken only by the bright flashes of the strobe lights. A sultry salsa beat pounded out of the speaker system, the heavy bass making the floor beneath his feet vibrate, and down on the dance floor, couples grinded together to the music. One of the couples was Garrett and Shelby, only they weren't doing much dancing. Just standing in the middle of the floor, making out as if they were the only two people in the room.

Next to Carson, fellow SEAL Ryan Evans tapped one hand on the iron railing and frowned at the display of vertical sex happening below.

"Shit, I really need to get laid," Ryan grumbled. He took a swig of beer, then slammed the bottle back on the table they'd been standing around for the past hour. Glancing over at the long chrome bar counter behind them, he frowned again. "And if anyone fucking suggests I hop into bed with one of those old dudes by the bar, I'll kick your ass."

Matt O'Connor laughed. "The bald one's kinda cute. I bet he'd do you."

"The only person I want to do is the maid of honor," Ryan said with a sigh. "Man, I'd give up my favorite rifle for a chance with her."

All the guys nodded, their gazes glumly moving in the direction of the sexy woman who was chatting with her husband near the bar. Brianna Holliday, the maid of honor, was the stuff of wet dreams. Tall, blonde and stacked. Her blue dress was knee-length, with a modest neckline, yet it just screamed "Fuck Me Now". No doubt that's what her husband was gonna do the second he got her home tonight. If Carson had a woman like that, he'd never let her get out of bed.

He turned back to his teammates. "Isn't it the duty of the best man to screw the maid of honor? Why am I deprived of the privilege?"

"Because you've already screwed the bride," Junior Lieutenant Will Charleston pointed out, finally joining the conversation.

Carson stifled a groan. Why wasn't he surprised that Will knew about his romp with Shelby and Garrett? He'd only told Matt, but when you spent all your time with the same five guys, secrets didn't stay secret for long.

"I wish I screwed the bride," Ryan said, staring longingly at Shelby.

Carson followed the other man's gaze, and couldn't help admiring Shelby himself. Shel was the epitome of a California girl—blonde hair, blue eyes, toned bod. And amazing in bed, too. Made him come so hard he could barely walk afterwards. Unfortunately, thinking about the threesome he'd had with Shelby and Garrett during that heat wave six months ago was a no-no. Now that the couple was getting married, it wasn't appropriate to picture his best friend's future wife naked.

"Quit acting like you're starved for sex," Matt said to Ryan. "Didn't you go home with that redhead from the bar last weekend?"

Ryan groaned. "Unfortunately. We went back to her place, and I was on the receiving end of a pretty awesome blowjob—and then her husband came home. I barely got out of there with my skin intact."

Matt hooted, Carson chuckled, and even Will, who rarely smiled, looked like he was fighting back laughter. Ry's story didn't come as a surprise to anyone, though. One of these days Ryan Evans was going to find himself on the receiving end of an ass kicking. He seemed to attract the married ones like flies to a corpse.

"Your dick's really gonna get you in trouble, you know that?" Matt said, voicing Carson's thoughts.

"At least I'm using my dick. Unlike you monks over here." He gestured to Will and Carson.

Carson raised a brow. "Don't go dragging me into this. My dick's doing fine, thank you very much."

"Good to hear," a throaty female voice remarked.

He swiveled his head in the direction of the voice, just in time to see a petite brunette in a yellow halter-top emerge from the shadows. The second floor of the club had a loft feel to it, a huge open space with a handful of floor-to-ceiling beams, and the brunette must have been leaning against one of those pillars, because Carson hadn't even seen her approach. Which raised the question, just how long had she been lurking in the darkness, eavesdropping on them?

The others looked as startled as he felt to see her standing there. "So, which one of you is going to dance with me?" she asked in that husky voice.

Man, how did a tiny thing like her have such a sexy, fuck-me voice? Carson studied her, waiting for flashes from the strobe to illuminate her face so he could get a better look. Each time a streak of light lit up her face, he liked what he saw. She had one of those faces you saw in makeup ads—smooth creamy skin, a small upturned nose, and naturally red lips that were lush and sensual and ridiculously kissable. He lowered his gaze and liked what he saw there too. Perky breasts, small but in proportion to her petite frame. She couldn't have been taller than five feet, but her sexy little body was a total turn-on.

The biggest turn-on about her was that he could see her nipples poking against her halter. Yup, she wasn't wearing a bra.

He noticed his teammates checking her out as well, saw their appreciation, and an odd pang of possessiveness gripped his insides.

"Well?" she prompted.

Well, what? Right, the dance. Carson quickly moved his gaze away from those small, tantalizing breasts and took a step forward before any of his friends—mainly Ryan—snatched up this hot little pixie.

"Sweetheart, I would love to dance with you," he drawled, shooting her his trademark ladies' man grin.

Women always told him that grin was hot enough to melt a glacier, and sure enough, he saw the brunette's cheeks redden a little. It could've been the shadows making her look flushed, but he preferred to think the smile had done it.

A pair of catlike green eyes focused on him. Shit, she had nice eyes. They tilted up just slightly at the corners, giving her an exotic air. "Let's do it, then."

Oh, he wanted to do it, all right. Although he'd never admit it to Ryan I-Need-To-Get-Laid Evans, it'd been way too long since Carson had slept with anyone. Five weeks, to be exact, and he was getting real tired of flying solo. The three-week mission in Colombia played a part in his current celibate status, but after that he had no excuse other than he simply hadn't encountered a woman who set his body on fire.

Six months ago, he might've settled for the first available warm body, but ever since his best friend had fallen for Shelby, Carson found it was getting harder to justify screwing random chicks. Garrett and Shelby were so disgustingly in love, they made him feel sleazy about his casual lifestyle. Not that he was looking for true love or anything, but lately he was pickier about who he fell into bed with.

He might, however, make an exception for the woman who'd just asked him to dance.

She walked ahead of him, and Carson took the opportunity to admire the way her short black skirt hugged her firm little bottom. He usually went for curvy and leggy, but something about this woman's fragile figure made his blood heat up.

He tore his eyes away from her delectable ass and followed her down the open spiral staircase leading to the main level. When she reached the bottom step, she cocked her head to check if he was still there, and when their gazes connected he saw a sensual smile tug on her pouty lips. Damn, those lips belonged in an X-rated video. Preferably one that featured him and the lips in question wrapped around his dick.

Amusement danced in her green eyes. "You're staring at my mouth."

"You've got a nice mouth," he answered glibly.

"So do you." She studied him. "In fact, you've got a nice everything. Are you an actor?"

"Male model," he lied, because he didn't feel like telling her he was a Navy SEAL.

Women had a tendency to go a little nutty when they found out what he did. They got all wide-eyed as fantasies of being swept off their feet by a real-life hero filled their pretty heads. And Carson had no desire to sweep anyone off her feet tonight, unless it involved sweeping this appealing brunette to the nearest bed.

She smiled again, but the look on her face said she didn't quite believe him. "Interesting. Do you pose in the nude?"

"All the time." He curled his fingers over her arm and led her toward the packed dance floor. The music was a lot louder down here, so he dipped his head to her ear and added, "I could give you a private show if you'd like."

She laughed, the sound quickly swallowed by the reggae song that pounded out of the speakers. Leaning up on her tiptoes, she brushed her lips over his ear as she said, "First you can dance with me, then I'll decide if I want to see you naked."

Carson grinned and pulled her into the throng of people. She immediately pressed her body to his and started to move. Those curvy breasts teased his chest, sending sparks of heat to his cock every time her small, erect nipples pushed against him. The top of her head barely reached his chin, and her soft wavy hair tickled his neck. She smelled like flowers and honey, the aroma filling his nostrils, subtle and yet far more potent than the scent of sweat, perfume and aftershave mingling in the hot air of the club.

He rested his hands on her tucked-in waist, slipping them under the hem of her halter-top so he could feel her bare skin. As he moved his body to the rhythm, he slid his fingers over her warm flesh, enjoying the silky feel of it. She sighed, her breath tickling his collarbone and searing right through his black T-shirt.

"How am I doing so far?" he asked.

She tilted her head up to look at him, a tiny smile playing on her lips. "So far, so good." She punctuated the words by rubbing her lower body against his pelvis.

His cock rose to attention, thickening to a long ridge that strained against the zipper of his jeans. Never missing a beat, he spun her around, then pressed his erection against her ass, running his hands up and down her bare arms.

He lowered his head to her ear again. "What's your name, sweetheart?"

"Jessica."

"I'm Carson." Then, unable to help it, he slid his tongue over the shell of her ear before sucking on the delicate lobe. "It's a pleasure to meet you, Jessica."

She pushed her butt out and rubbed it over his erection before spinning back around and wrapping her arms around his neck. Their gazes locked, and the hint of sex sizzled in the air between them. Actually, scratch that. He would definitely be having sex with this green-eyed seductress tonight, no *hint* about it.

She obviously shared the sentiment, because the next thing he knew she was kissing him.

Her hot mouth latched onto his, her eager tongue darting out and filling his mouth.

Oh *yeah*.

Carson didn't care that they were in the middle of a crowded dance floor, didn't care that this was his best friend's stag or that his buddies were probably getting a kick out of watching him from the second-floor railing. All he cared about was devouring every inch of sweet Jessica's mouth. And devour he did.

He thrust one hand into her long, wavy hair and angled her head for better access, shoving his tongue deep in her mouth. She tasted like alcohol and sex. His erection pulsed as she flicked her tongue over his, over and over again, and then she nibbled on his bottom lip and his cock damn well near exploded. *Jesus.* He was harder than a slab of marble, and in serious danger of coming in his pants from one—albeit very erotic—kiss.

"Let's get out of here," he muttered against her lips, shaping her ass with his hands and thrusting his aching groin against her belly.

"No, I want you now." She kissed him again, long and hard, moving one hand down his chest and palming the bulge in his jeans.

He almost keeled over backwards. A groan rose in his throat and it took all his willpower to move her hand away. "We're on the dance floor, sweetheart," he pointed out.

She shot him a wicked smile. "So?"

Christ, this woman was going to kill him. He'd never been more turned on in his twenty-nine years, and he suddenly knew that if he didn't fuck her—*now*—he really would explode in his pants.

"C'mere," he ordered gruffly, grabbing her hand and leading her out of the mob of dancers.

He had no fucking clue where he was taking her. He just walked as fast as he could—difficult seeing as the Erection of the Year was dominating his lower body. He shoved random people out of his way, not bothering with *excuse me*, just pushing forward. In the darkness, he caught sight of a corridor leading toward the restrooms. Both the men's and ladies' rooms had a line. Goddammit.

Still gripping Jessica's hand, he looked around, spotted a door marked *Supplies* and pushed at the handle with his other hand.

A dark closet welcomed them, lined with cleaning items and toilet paper and smelling of pine, lemon and rubbing alcohol.

Carson barely noticed his surroundings. He locked the door behind them, promptly shoved Jessica against the wall, and kissed her again. She instantly parted her lips and sought out his tongue, lapping at it like an impatient kitten in front of a saucer of milk. There was something desperate about her kiss, and when he pulled back and looked into her eyes, he saw a flicker of desperation there, too.

"You okay?" he murmured, caressing her lower back with one hand. The heat of her skin was driving him crazy, making it difficult to think, let alone talk.

"I'm fine. Great, actually. No, better than great." Her voice trembled slightly, but her gaze now shone with passion and determination. She wrapped her arms around his neck and ran her fingers along his jaw. "I need you to do something for me, Carson."

It was hard to concentrate with her stroking his face like that, but he managed to ask, "What is it?"

"I need you to rock my world. Can you do that for me?"

The words were laced with steely fortitude and teasing challenge, and again, that twinge of desperation. He got the feeling something was up with her. That she was upset, or pissed off—trying to get back at an ex, perhaps? Maybe, but at this point, he didn't care. She wanted her world rocked? Well, he was definitely the man for that job.

He pulled his wallet from his pocket and retrieved the condom he kept there. Jessica's eyes darkened with passion when she saw the foil wrapper. While he unwrapped it, she rubbed the front of his jeans, up and down, down and up, until his cock ached so badly he could barely suck in a breath. Then she unzipped his pants and wrapped her fingers around his erection.

"You're so hard," she whispered as she stroked him, swirling one finger over his swollen tip.

"All because of you, sweetheart," he rasped out, finally managing to roll the damn condom onto his throbbing shaft. "Take your panties off."

For a second she looked nervous. Then she slipped her hands underneath her skirt and slowly peeled her silky black underwear down her legs. She kicked them aside, watching him expectantly. "Any more demands?" she asked with a grin.

"Just one." He moved closer and gripped her hips with both hands. "Wrap your legs around me."

She did as she was told, and a second later he was cupping her warm ass in his hands and lifting her up. He would've liked to drop to his knees and lick her up like an ice cream cone, get her nice and wet for him, but she didn't seem interested in foreplay. And it wasn't necessary, he soon learned, as he slid his cock deep inside her and found himself surrounded by her tight, soaked pussy. He nearly keeled over backwards, relying on all his strength to keep them both upright and not pass out from the incredible sensations.

"God, you feel good," he choked out, burying his face in the crook of her neck.

She responded by clasping her legs tighter around him and squeezing his cock with her inner muscles. And just like that, he lost control. Not that he'd been in control to begin with. Oh no, he'd said goodbye to his control the second this woman walked up to him, the second she latched her mouth on his and asked him to rock her world.

"Fuck me, damn it," she moaned, pressing her lips to his shoulder.

There it was, that desperation again. And yet again, he didn't care.

Instead, he started to thrust, plunging his cock into her as hard as he could, as fast as he could. There was no stopping this. Whatever this was. A sexual hurricane. A moment of crazy, blind, uncontrollable lust. He fucked her against the wall, rough and wild, and she loved every minute of it.

"Yes, oh my God, *yes.*"

Her soft cries, mingled with dirty commands and breathy moans, drove him out of his mind. He dug his fingers into her ass, pumping in and out of that sweet, sopping-wet paradise, unable to slow down, not even for a second.

"More," she said between moans, rocking hard against him.

He bent down and shoved his tongue in her mouth, kissing her senseless while he continued thrusting into her as deep as he could go. Her lips trembled beneath his, her fingers curled around his neck, and when he angled her body so that his cock brushed over her clit each time he withdrew, she gave a wild cry and exploded against him.

Her orgasm was too much for him. The way her pussy clamped around his cock, her sexy moans, the sheer bliss in her green eyes—he toppled right over the edge with her, coming so hard his balls burned with the agonizing force of the pleasure. His breath came out ragged, his heart pounding so hard he could hear nothing but the sound it made as it thudded against his ribcage.

They stayed there for a moment, leaning against the wall, breathing hard, their bodies joined together, until finally she slid off him without a word.

Carson swallowed, unable to comprehend what had happened. He'd just had the best sex of his life, in a supply closet of a nightclub, with a woman he'd known for all of five minutes. What the hell was up with that?

He reached down and removed the condom from his still aching erection, watching as Jessica bent to pick up her panties. She quickly put them on, smoothed out the front of her skirt and reached up to run her shaky hands through her dark hair.

"So…" he began, then trailed off, unsure of what to say.

She gazed up at him with a strange little smile, her green eyes flickering with dazed pleasure and what looked like a touch of uncertainty.

"Thank you," she finally said.

Before he could tell her she had absolutely nothing to thank him for—hell, he should be thanking *her*—she unlocked the door and darted out of the supply closet.

He stared at the door, stupefied. What the hell just happened?

Chapter One

One Month Later

Although he truly hated weddings, Carson had to admit that Garrett and Shelby had done a pretty good job with theirs. The altar had been set up only a few yards from the shoreline of Coronado Beach, white roses twining around the little structure's intricate cedar frame. The bride looked like an angel sent from heaven, her blonde hair a halo illuminated by the setting sun. The groom wore his pristine Navy dress whites, and the happy couple only had eyes for each other as the preacher spoke in an easy, jovial tone that added some liveliness to the ceremony.

Carson wondered if the preacher would still feel jovial if he knew the best man had slept with the bride. While the groom watched.

Probably not a tidbit he should mention at the reception, he decided as he smothered a grin and handed the silver wedding band to Garrett.

Garrett accepted the ring with visibly trembling fingers and Carson tried not to raise a brow. He'd never seen his best friend's hands shake. Ever. The two men had been part of the same SEAL team for four years now, and in the life of a Navy SEAL, shaky hands usually equaled instant death. Good thing Garrett was steadier with a weapon than he was with a wedding ring.

"I, John, take you, Shelby…"

Shit, how was it possible that his best friend was getting married? Garrett had proposed to Shelby months ago, they'd been planning the wedding for ages, yet it hadn't seemed real to Carson until just now. And the realization brought with it a wave of unease. He and Garrett had always been the ultimate bachelors. When they weren't on assignment, they'd painted the town every color known to man. Scored with numerous chicks. Engaged in some wild threesomes.

Who'd he do that with now?

And did he even *want* to?

Ever since the night at the Hot Zone, he'd been wondering if maybe it was time to say goodbye to the casual lifestyle. He had the mysterious Jessica to thank for that, of course. She'd left him in that closet, harder than ever, and wondering if he'd dreamed it all—something he still wasn't entirely sure of, seeing as he'd searched the entire nightclub for her and come up empty-handed. At first he was upset to discover she was really gone, but after a while he'd grown angry. At himself.

When had he become such a sleaze? It was one thing to have casual affairs with women he knew, but to fuck a complete stranger in a supply closet? When had he become *that guy*, the one who didn't care about anything but sticking his dick in the first available pussy?

The encounter had forced him to take a good look at himself, and his lifestyle. And now, watching Garrett and Shelby exchange their vows with such unadulterated love in their eyes, he suspected it might really be time to retire from the random sex scene and look for something more meaningful. He was twenty-nine years old, for Christ's sake. Wasn't it time to grow up? Have a relationship that lasted more than five minutes in the closet of a nightclub?

"I, Shelby, take you, John, to be my lawfully wedded husband..."

Carson lifted his head, forcing himself to quit wallowing and focus on the vows being exchanged. But a second later his peripheral vision caught a flash of movement and he became distracted again.

He shifted his head ever so slightly, seeking out what had snagged his attention. A short brunette stood a few yards away, next to the long buffet table that had been set up for the reception. Her back was half turned, so he only caught a glimpse of her profile, but the black skirt and white blouse she wore told him she was part of the catering staff.

Question was—why did one of the catering staff have her hand down her own shirt?

And was that fondling going on under there?

Carson studied the strange display. No, not fondling. Looked like she was fumbling with...a bra strap? Her hair fell onto her face like a curtain, further shielding her features from him, as she fiddled with the bra.

He squinted. Then choked back a laugh when he realized what was happening. The girl's bra strap had ripped—and she was attempting to tie the two ends together.

Priceless.

He couldn't help it. A chuckle slid out of his throat.

Unfortunately, the chuckle came out at the exact moment the preacher demanded to know if anyone had a reason why the bride and groom shouldn't be together.

Garrett and Shelby instantly swiveled their heads in his direction, shock clearly etched in their faces.

"What? No," Carson said quickly, keeping his voice low. He turned to the preacher. "No. I'm not speaking. I'm forever holding my peace. These two belong together. Please, just go on."

"I'm going to kick your ass for this," Garrett muttered before turning his attention back to the ceremony.

Shelby just glared at him.

Fuck. Wonderful. Now everyone and their mother would think Carson objected to this union. Damn caterer and her broken bra.

He forced himself not to glance in that direction again, instead concentrating on the end of the ceremony and then applauding after Garrett and Shelby locked lips. The newly married couple walked down the sandy aisle, hand-in-hand, and were immediately swarmed by well-wishers and teary-eyed relatives.

Carson shoved his hands in the pockets of his crisp white Navy uniform and followed the rest of the wedding party down the aisle. As they headed for the reception area, he glanced over at the buffet and sought out the bra-challenged waitress.

There she was. Talking to a curly-haired blonde and gesturing wildly.

His eyes narrowed as she suddenly turned her head.

That face…green eyes…pouty lips…

Jesus, he *knew* that face.

He took a few steps closer, bewildered, a bit angry, still focused on the familiar pixie-esque features, the long brown hair, the round little ass…

The brunette grabbed the other waitress's arm and proceeded to drag her toward the steps leading away from the beach. A second later, the two were out of sight.

But not before Carson caught another glimpse of her face, which confirmed what he already knew.

The mysterious Jessica had made another appearance.

And this time, there was no damn way he was letting her get away from him again.

"WHAT AM I GOING TO DO?" HOLLY LAWSON WAILED, WAVING HER RIPPED bra around like a matador taunting an irate bull.

Zoe Shickler grinned. "You go without, that's what you do."

"This shirt is white, Zoe. And it's see-through. Vanessa will freak."

"Vanessa will be too busy bustling around and making sure the guests are enjoying themselves to notice her assistant's tits."

"I'll notice! And so will all those Navy guys. In an hour or so they'll all be plastered and making cracks about my nipples."

"So? If you're lucky, maybe one of them will offer to suckle you for a bit." Zoe's grin widened. "Did you see the best man?" She promptly began fanning herself.

"I've been too busy setting up the buffet to notice the best man, Zoe. And this isn't a joke," Holly grumbled. "I can't serve drinks topless."

"You're wearing a shirt, for God's sake." Zoe rolled her eyes and rose from the cab of the pickup truck she'd been sitting on. "Come on, we should head back. I shouldn't have let you drag me here to begin with. *That* Vanessa will freak about."

Holly sighed. "You go ahead. I need time to gather my courage."

She watched as the other waitress crossed the gravel parking lot and headed for the narrow concrete staircase that led down to the beach. The lot was crammed with cars, all belonging to the sixty or so people who would soon get a very candid eyeful of Holly Lawson's braless breasts.

God, this entire day had been a disaster from the second she'd opened her eyes. She'd woken up to the shrill ringing of her phone, answered it to hear the shrill voice of her older sister, and proceeded to spend the morning re-dyeing Caroline's hair after her sister had *accidentally* dyed it purple the night before. Apparently there'd been some sort of communication breakdown between Caroline and her Korean hairdresser, but who the hell knew. Despite the fact that she was twenty-nine—*five* years older than Holly—Caroline always seemed to get herself in one mess after the other. Somehow Holly was the one who got stuck cleaning it.

And she didn't even want to get started on the rest of her siblings. Twenty-five-year-old Todd was as scatterbrained as Caroline, as well as the other reason she'd had such a crappy day—he'd forgotten he had a college exam to write tomorrow morning and coerced Holly into spending the afternoon quizzing him. And after she'd left Todd's dorm, her eldest brother Kyle called with an emergency of his own. He'd locked himself out of his car and needed her to drive over with the spare keys. Her keychain was heavier than a brick, thanks to all the spare keys she had clipped to it, all belonging to her idiot siblings who couldn't seem to do anything for themselves.

Holly was the baby of the family. She was only twenty-four, damn it. How had she been dubbed the Lawson family janitor?

Now, thanks to her siblings' crisis, she was going to have to waitress an entire wedding without a bra. When she'd been getting dressed, she'd noticed that the bra strap was fraying a little, but there hadn't been time to change because she was already running late. So she'd hightailed it out of her apartment, sped over to this wedding, and what happened twenty minutes into it? Her bra broke.

She hated her life. She really, truly did. She was sick of taking care of everyone in her family, sick of working as a waitress when what she really wanted to do was have a restaurant of her own, and sick of getting dumped.

Oh no, change brain direction now, Holly, before you think about—
Steve.

And yep, she was thinking about Steve,

She'd told herself she wasn't allowed to anymore, but for the past month, thoughts of her ex had constantly floated into her head. It truly sucked when the person you were madly in love with broke your heart. She'd thought he was her soul mate. He worked as a sous-chef at an Italian restaurant, created his own recipes in his spare time, and rode a seriously sexy Harley. She'd envisioned the two of them working together, owning a restaurant, having sex on the back of his motorcycle, getting married, and moving out of state so she didn't have to see her family.

Instead, she'd gotten dumped. And why? Because Steve didn't like the fact that she had other responsibilities that didn't involve, well, fucking on the back of his Harley. In no uncertain terms, he'd told her to choose—him or everything else in her life. The selfishness of his demand still grated. How could she have been so wrong about him?

Of course, one good thing had come out of the break-up, but she wasn't allowed to think about *that*, either.

Nope. Because then she'd have to admit that the highlight of her sad, pathetic little life had been wild, sweaty sex in a closet with a complete stranger. And if that's all a girl had to be proud of, she seriously needed a new life.

Straightening her shoulders, Holly finally forced herself to quit sulking. She glanced ruefully at the bra in her hand before stuffing it in the wide front pocket of her black apron. Then she sighed again, pushed her hair behind her ears, and headed back to the beach.

When she stepped onto the sand, the reception was already in full swing. Tables had been set up on the beach, the chairs occupied by wedding guests digging into the seafood spread Holly had spent most of last night preparing. Since it was a buffet, the guests were in charge of getting their own food, but the catering staff was responsible for serving drinks, so Holly quickly headed for the bar area.

The sun was only a sliver of pink and yellow in the horizon, but it was still hot out, hot enough to make her white shirt cling to her skin. Great, soon she'd look like a contestant in a wet T-shirt contest. The bride and groom would be thrilled.

"So, did you calm down?" Zoe asked, strolling up to the bar and loading her tray with glasses of champagne.

"If you mean am I happy about the fact that you can see my nipples through this shirt, then no, I haven't calmed down," she replied. "But I'll deal with it, don't worry."

"Good." Zoe grinned. "And you get to deal with it while bringing some beers over to the hottie table. Vanessa said I can't serve them anymore, because apparently I spend too much time flirting."

"Where exactly is the hottie table?"

Zoe's blue eyes twinkled as she slanted her head to the left. Holly followed her coworker's gaze. The hottie table *indeed*. Four ridiculously attractive men in Navy dress whites sat there, each one more handsome than the next. Like that blond one. Man, there was something unbelievably appealing about that chiseled, GQ face and broad shoulders and—

The color drained from her face.

"Oh my God," she blurted out, nearly dropping the tray she'd just stacked with beer bottles.

Zoe giggled and tossed her curly hair over her shoulder. "I know, right? It's like an orgasmic feast over there."

Holly's cheeks went from white to red. Oh *shit*. Was it actually him or was she hallucinating? Because what were the odds of running into her one-night-stand *here*, at a wedding she was waitressing at?

Obviously pretty good, because the guy's head suddenly swiveled in her direction as if he sensed her presence, and then those deep blue eyes were fixed on her. All doubts flew from her mind. It was him. Her hunk from the Hot Zone. The guy she'd jumped four hours after Steve had dumped her.

"Male model, my ass," she muttered, though a part of her wasn't surprised to discover he was in the Navy. She hadn't quite bought his model story anyway.

Zoe gave her a blank look. "Huh?"

"The guy. The blond." Her voice dropped to a whisper. "Remember I told you about the guy I hooked up with a month ago, at the club? Well, that's *him*."

Delight lit up Zoe's eyes. "Seriously?"

"Yep."

Embarrassment heated her face as she thought about that night. She'd gone to the Hot Zone with Caroline, who'd dragged Holly out after finding her in her apartment crying over Steve. Holly hadn't wanted to go, yet somehow her sister had convinced her they'd have a good time. But ten minutes after they walked into the club, Caroline disappeared with a tall, Latin heartthrob and Holly had found herself alone.

She'd stood in the shadows, trying not to think about Steve, trying not to cry, and that's when she'd overheard those guys talking. About sex. About needing to get laid. Normally she thought those types of men were sleazy, but at that moment, she'd found herself wondering, what would be so bad about sleeping with someone she didn't know? What would be so terrible about using another man to distract herself from how much Steve had hurt her?

She'd never had a one-night-stand in her life, and if Steve hadn't ended things so abruptly and left her so distraught, she might not have even considered it. But that night, it seemed like a good idea. So she'd walked up to the guys, asked one to dance, and before she knew it, she'd transformed into someone else.

She wasn't responsible, stressed out Holly Lawson anymore. She was *Jessica*. Jessica, who didn't clean up her family's messes or work too hard or get dumped. Jessica did whatever the hell she wanted, *whoever* the hell she wanted, and consequences be damned.

Unfortunately, she wasn't Jessica, was she? Nope, she was Holly. And in Holly's life, there were always consequences.

Case in point—the man staring at her from across the sand.

"Holly, this is awesome," Zoe gushed, jerking her out of her thoughts. "He's so freaking hot, I'm getting turned on just looking at him. I can't believe the two of you hooked up! Give me details, girl!"

Holly had no intention of revealing anything, and fortunately she didn't have to, because Vanessa, the owner of the catering company, was signaling the two waitresses to get back to work.

Unfortunately, getting back to work meant having to deliver the tray of beers to the hottie table, where she'd have to look into the eyes of the man she'd fucked in a closet and explain why she'd run out on him.

Which only confirmed what she'd already accepted years ago—when it came to her life, she could never catch a break.

Chapter Two

"Is it just me or can you totally see through that waitress's shirt?" Ryan asked, his gaze glued to the brunette who approached their table with very reluctant steps.

Carson couldn't tear his gaze from her, either. He still couldn't believe she was actually here. Obviously she worked for the catering company, but a part of him couldn't help wondering if fate was responsible. Hadn't he just decided that it was time to seek out something more meaningful when it came to women?

Well, who better to explore it with than the woman he'd had the best sex of his life with?

"Oh, I can definitely see through her shirt," Matt agreed with a grin. "And I most certainly like what I'm seeing."

"Hey…" Ryan squinted. "Shit, that's the girl from the club." He immediately stared at Carson. "Didn't you—" He stopped abruptly as Jessica reached the table.

Although she was as pretty as Carson remembered, she looked nothing like the sexy seductress who'd rubbed herself against him on the dance floor. This Jessica seemed shyer, more wholesome, and his curiosity was instantly piqued.

"Hi," she said, awkwardly standing in front of them with a tray full of beers in her hands. "Are you boys having a nice time?"

"We are now," Ryan muttered, his eyes never leaving her chest.

Carson felt a spark of irritation. Yeah, you could see the outline of her nipples perfectly through that thin white blouse, but he didn't like that Ryan was ogling her. Jessica deserved more respect than that.

He locked his gaze with hers and smiled faintly. "Good to see you again, Jessica."

She swallowed, her cheeks reddening. "Um, yeah, you too…um…"

"Carson," he filled in, bristling. She didn't even remember his goddamn name?

"I remember," she said, obviously reading his mind. Her hands trembled as she started lifting bottles off her tray and setting them down on the table.

Carson ignored the beer she placed in front of him, his eyes never leaving hers. Her nervousness practically radiated from her pores, and he could tell she was both embarrassed and uncomfortable. He wanted to say something, ask her why she'd hurried off that night, ask her if they could talk when the reception ended, but all of his friends were watching him curiously and he couldn't seem to form any words.

A short silence fell, until Jessica finally cleared her throat and said, "Um, okay, so I'll be back in a while to check on you guys." Then she hurried off like a scared bunny.

Another silence.

"Well. That was awkward," Will said dryly. He reached for his beer and took a sip. "What exactly happened at the club that night, man?"

"Nothing," Carson muttered.

He hadn't told any of the guys about the closet fuck. The encounter had totally messed him up, made him reevaluate his lifestyle, and he hadn't wanted to talk about it with anyone, especially guys like Ryan and Matt, who were still so hooked on the notion of casual sex.

"Nothing?" Ryan echoed. "Then you won't mind if I ask her out, right? Because, fuck, she is *hot*."

Carson clenched his fists. "Don't even think about it."

"That's what I thought." Ryan grinned. "Nothing, my ass."

HE WAS WATCHING HER AGAIN. HOLLY COULD FEEL HIS EYES ON HER AS she handed a glass of red wine to the mother of the bride. She had to force herself not to turn her head. Lord, that gaze was burning her up. Her skin felt so hot she was tempted to sprint toward the waves and dive in, but she doubted the cold water would lower her body temperature. He'd been sending those sizzling glances her way for *three* hours and she was past the point of cooling down. She was so turned on she could barely breathe.

She knew he wanted to talk to her. She could see it every time she delivered another tray of beers to his table. Each time she walked over there, he just stared at her with those killer blue eyes, a million questions on his face.

Well, she didn't want to answer any questions. Wasn't the point of one-night-stands that you weren't supposed to make excuses? She'd been upset that night, she'd wanted to forget about Steve, so she'd propositioned a stranger and had sex with him in a closet. Then she'd crashed down to earth after a spectacular orgasm, realized what she'd done, become mortified and ran away. Why couldn't they just leave it at that?

And why wouldn't her clit stop throbbing, damn it? It was getting hard to walk with that ache between her legs.

Mercifully, the party was dwindling. Most of the guests had wished the bride and groom well and headed out. Even the happy couple had left. The only people who remained were a few couples laughing over wine, and the four SEALS.

Zoe walked over to her. "Vanessa said to start packing up."

"Thank God. My feet are killing me."

They headed over to the buffet area. Holly spent the next twenty minutes wrapping up the leftovers, gathering empty bottles, and making countless trips to and from the catering van. When she finally finished, she was relieved to find that everyone was gone. The tables on the beach had been folded up, the guests had taken off, and only catering staff remained.

Her sexy SEAL was nowhere to be seen, which obviously meant he didn't care enough to question *Jessica* and had decided to call it a night.

That should have been a relief, and yet a part of her was a little disappointed. Carson was probably the best-looking man she'd ever met in her life. Definitely the best lay of her life—not that she had a lot to compare him to. She'd only slept with two other men—Steve, and a boy she'd dated in her senior year of high school.

She shouldn't care that Carson had left. They were nothing more than a couple of strangers who happened to have sex one night. She didn't know him. He didn't know her.

But...

Damn it, she'd liked the way she'd felt that night with him. She'd liked being Jessica, not thinking about how much she disliked her life, not worrying about having to take care of anyone but herself. She'd been in control, lived for the moment, seized the pleasure.

Tonight, with Carson sitting at that table watching her all night, she'd felt that way again. She'd forgotten about being late for work, about her stupid broken bra, about everything but the fact that a really sexy man was undressing her with his eyes.

Oh well. She was foolish to think he could actually have been interested in her. She was too short, her boobs too small, her personality too sarcastic. Normally it didn't bother her. Because along with all those other irritating *toos*, she was also too busy cleaning up her family's messes and helping them with their even messier love lives to care about her own.

"I'm heading out," Zoe called. "You coming?"

Holly walked over to her friend. "I think I'll stick around for a bit longer. I have a feeling if I go home I'll find a dozen SOS messages on my machine from the delinquents."

Zoe sighed. "You've got to stop letting your family dominate your life, Hol. You're twenty-four. You should be having fun, enjoying your hotness and screwing tons of guys."

At the moment, everything Zoe said sounded like pure and total heaven. Too bad it wasn't going to happen. With her job, her family, and the culinary course she was taking, it was tough enough finding time to eat, let alone screw.

"You going to be okay out here alone?" Zoe asked, gesturing to the deserted stretch of beach.

"I've got my cell and my pepper spray. I'll be fine."

Zoe leaned forward and gave her a quick hug. "I'll see you Sunday at the Grier wedding."

Holly watched her friend disappear up the steps leading to the lot, then turned around and walked toward the shoreline. She kicked off her sandals, dug her toes into the sand and breathed in the warm night air. She loved the ocean. Nothing relaxed her more than the sight of the waves lapping against the shore and the sound of gulls squawking as they soared over the calm, turquoise water.

But tonight, not even her favorite view could make her feel better. She should've pulled Carson aside and talked to him. She'd served his table all evening. She'd seen him staring at her. Seen the undisguised interest and curiosity in his eyes. The *lust*. And instead of doing something about it, she'd kept walking up to him like a robot, handing him a beer and hurrying away. No wonder she had no luck with men. These days a woman needed to be proactive, not scurry away like a skittish animal whenever a hot guy looked at her.

The sound of footsteps put an end to her self-pity party. She figured it was someone from the catering company who'd forgotten something, but when she turned around, her gaze collided with a pair of sexy blue eyes.

Carson was back.

He strode up to her, his muscles rippling beneath the dress whites he wore. What was it about a man in uniform that never failed to make a woman's heart pound?

"You're still here," he said, then winced as if he hated that he'd stated the obvious. "I was waiting for you in the parking lot. I got worried when you didn't show."

Holly's pulse sped up. "You were waiting for me?"

He raked a hand through his dirty-blond hair. "We never got a chance to, um, catch up. And I was going to offer you a ride home."

"I have a car." *I have a car?* That's all she could come up with? How about, *I'm sorry I left you in a supply closet after you gave me the best orgasm of my life?*

"Okay. Then let's just do the catching up then." He offered a small smile. "So how've you been, Jessica?"

Jessica. Now there was a nice splash of reality if she'd ever heard one.

"That's...um...kind of not my name," she confessed.

"It's not your name," he repeated flatly.

"No."

"You lied?"

"Yes."

"Why?" he demanded.

"I..." She released a long breath. "I wasn't in the best state of mind that night. I'd just gotten dumped by my boyfriend, and then my sister dragged me to a club, and I was upset and tired of my life, tired of *me*." She gave a rueful shrug. "I guess I just wanted to be someone else for the night."

"Do you do that often, pretend to be someone else?" There was a touch of sarcasm to his voice. "How many other guys have you seduced and then deserted?"

She sighed. "You were the first."

"I see."

It was obvious from the skeptical look in his blue eyes that he totally *didn't* see, but she didn't feel like explaining herself further. Yes, she'd lied. Yes, she'd seduced him. But he sure hadn't been complaining when she'd thrown herself at him, had he? Oh no. He'd been right there with her, groping her ass and dragging her into the closet for a sexual tryst. He hadn't even known her, for Pete's sake. Any guy who had sex with a random stranger wasn't one to judge.

Carson must've reached the same conclusion as her, because the sarcastic glint left his eyes and suddenly he cast her a sexy grin. "It was a pretty fun time, wasn't it?"

Fun? Talk about the understatement of the year. Before she could stop it, memories of that night rushed back to her. How warm and firm Carson's lips had felt pressed against her own. The hardness of his chest under her fingers. His thick cock sliding deep inside her, making her cry out with pleasure. She'd never come so hard in her life, and just thinking about the orgasm caused her thighs to tremble.

God, she wanted to feel that way again. Wild and free and desirable.

"It was amazing," she corrected.

He smiled again, his eyes darkening seductively. "Definitely."

"Want to do it again?"

Oh boy—where had *that* come from? She immediately slammed her mouth closed, her cheeks heating with embarrassment.

Carson slanted his head, looking both intrigued and baffled, but he didn't respond, just stared at her for a moment as if trying to figure out if she was serious.

She took his silence as an opportunity to stare at *him*, and she liked everything she saw. He was so unbelievably attractive in that uniform. The white shirt molded to his broad, rippled chest, and the pants clung to his trim hips and long muscular legs, hugging his crotch in a way that revealed he was very much aroused.

She couldn't help it—she fixated on the long, thick ridge. As she remembered how perfectly he'd fit inside her, how well they'd moved together, the craziest urge overtook her. She wanted to touch him and stroke him and—

Her hand clearly had a mind of its own.

"Whoa," Carson murmured, his gaze instantly dropping south.

Holly ran her fingers over his tantalizing erection, lightly applying pressure with her palm and rubbing.

"You do realize—" he sucked in a breath, "—you're, uh, you know, you're doing *that*."

She blinked, snapping out of whatever sexual trance she'd fallen into and realizing what she was doing. She quickly withdrew her hand, her face scorching. "Oh gosh, I'm sorry. I just..." There were no words. No matter what she said, this man was going to think she was a sex-crazed psycho.

He released a choked laugh. "Is this a habit, touching men you hardly know?"

She turned away, so mortified she could barely breathe. What was the *matter* with her? She didn't normally behave this way with guys. Truth be told, she didn't have much experience with initiating sexual encounters. She didn't have much experience, period. Her life was too chaotic, and since she was always in control when it came to work and family, she'd always been happy letting the men in her life take control in the bedroom.

"I'm sorry," she said again, keeping her gaze on the waves lapping against the shore.

She heard his pants rustle as he moved closer, and then his fingers were touching her chin, turning it so she had no choice but to look at him. He studied her carefully. "Who are you?" he finally asked, his voice laced with intrigue. "What's your real name?"

She swallowed. "Holly. Holly Lawson."

Carson's mouth quirked. "Holly. Suits you better than Jessica." He stroked her jaw, his fingers so warm and gentle she almost purred in pleasure. "Why did you sleep with me the night at the club?"

"I already told you, I was upset. I wanted to forget."

"Forget what?"

"My ex." She let out a shaky breath. "Myself."

"Why on earth would you want to forget yourself?"

"Because…sometimes I get tired of myself," she blurted out. "I've been such a good girl all my life, Carson. I'm the perfect, obedient daughter, the perfect sister. I take care of everyone in my family—my brothers and sister, my dad, who can't even go grocery shopping on his own. My mom…she used to do everything, but…" She blinked back the tears stinging her eyelids. "She died two years ago."

"I'm sorry," Carson said softly, running his fingers along her cheek.

"Me too. I miss her. And after she died, I got cast into the Mom role. I'm the youngest, for God's sake, and yet somehow I have to take care of everyone else. So *that's* what I wanted to forget, okay? I just wanted one night where I didn't have to think about my family, or work, or being responsible and good. I wanted to be selfish and wild and *bad.*" Holly shook her head in irritation. "I still want that. And you being here makes me want it even more. The night with you was the best time I've had in so long."

She couldn't believe she was spilling her guts to him, but it felt good letting it all out. For two years she'd focused on making sure everyone in her family was happy, and she was tired of it. Why couldn't she think about her own happiness for once? What *she* wanted?

And perplexing as it was, what she wanted at the moment was Carson. She didn't know anything about him, only that he was in the Navy, he was drop-dead gorgeous, and he had the power to set her body on fire. Did she really need to know anything more?

A strange sense of liberation flooded her body as her brain informed her that no, she didn't. She was twenty-four years old. She was allowed to have a casual fling that didn't lead to a relationship. Because, at the moment, she didn't *want* a relationship. Her last one had left scars. Besides, she was busy with work, busy with culinary school, busy playing mother hen to her family.

But that didn't mean she had to be too busy for sex.

"I think…" She moistened her dry lips and met his gaze. "I think maybe we should have a fling."

He raised his eyebrows. "A fling?"

Uncertainty tugged at her belly. "An affair then? Friends with bennies? You know, not dating, but, um, spending a couple of weeks having sex…"

"So you want to have sex with me, but not date me?"

She nodded.

A pained expression creased his handsome face. "Well, then, that might be a problem."

She fought back disappointment. "Why?"

"Because I'm not really interested in flings anymore." Carson's jaw tensed. "After the night at the club, I decided I'm not that kind of guy anymore."

"What kind of guy?"

He frowned. "The kind who screws random strangers in closets." He shook his head, looking upset. "I've done the casual thing all my life and I think it's time to stop it." Something that resembled vulnerability flashed across his eyes. "I want to go on a date with you."

"What? Why?"

He shot her a cute grin. "Because I like you. You're...well, you're kind of weird."

She bristled. "Thanks."

"In a good way," he added quickly. "I mean, you're gorgeous, sure, but there's something else that draws me to you. Maybe it's that good girl image you're determined to lose. And you're funny, and interesting, and...I don't know, I just wouldn't mind getting to know you."

She had no response. It was really sweet, everything he was saying, but she wasn't sure she wanted sweet right now. The night she'd slept with Carson, she hadn't been sweet. Naughty, maybe. Reckless, sure. But not sweet.

And a date? That was the last thing she wanted right now. She'd just gotten out of a six-month relationship, one she'd poured so much time and energy into—for nothing. At the moment, dating again sounded way too tiring, and she was tired enough as it was. Sex, she could handle, but not a new romance. Not when her heart was still recovering from Steve.

"So what do you say?" Carson asked, looking oddly nervous.

She felt awful, but she had to tell the truth. "I don't want to start dating anyone right now. I recently got out of a relationship. I'm swamped with work and the culinary course I'm taking. I just want...sex."

He shoved his hands in his pockets and gave her a rueful look. "Then I'm sorry. I can't help you."

She rolled her eyes. "Sure you can. Just do me again."

A faint smile broke through the serious expression on his face, but it faded quickly. "I'm serious, Holly. I want something different this time around."

They'd reached an impasse. She could see it. But she could also see the glimmer of desire in his blue eyes.

Maybe if she gave him a tiny little push...

Licking her lips, she stepped forward and rested both palms on his impossibly broad shoulders. "Are you sure I can't change your mind?"

He was a lot taller than her and she had to tilt her head fully to look into his eyes. The desire she'd seen there deepened the moment she'd touched him.

Fueled by the obvious attraction, she leaned up on her tiptoes and brushed her lips over his.

For a second he didn't respond, but he didn't hold back for long—a moment later he parted her lips with his tongue and kissed the hell out of her. Heat rolled through her in waves, making her breasts tingle, her thighs ache. His mouth was warm and persuasive, his tongue so skilled she closed her eyes to savor each sensual stroke.

Carson's hands slid down her back to her ass, cupping it, stroking it, and then he moved one hand to her stomach, inched it down to the juncture of her thighs...and pulled it away.

She swallowed a groan of disappointment as he ended the incredible kiss.

"No." His features strained. "I meant what I said. I want more this time."

Holly could see that she'd lost the battle. Fortunately, the war was still up for grabs.

Sighing, she asked, "Do you have a cell phone?"

"Yeah. Why?"

"Can I see it?"

Shooting her a quizzical look, he pulled his phone from his back pocket and handed it to her. Without giving him time to object, she quickly programmed in her phone number and handed him back the cell.

"My number's in there now," she said with a grin. "If you change your mind, you know how to reach me."

Carson looked pained. "You really want this fling, huh?"

"You bet I do. So don't keep me waiting long, okay, Carson?"

Still grinning, she turned and walked away.

Chapter Three

"CAN YOU TELL ME WHY THE FUCK WE'RE PLAYING MINI-GOLF?" WILL asked as he awkwardly gripped his putter with two hands. Will, the SEAL who could jump off a helicopter with his eyes closed, stared at the hole in bewilderment, as if unable to comprehend why a fake mountain blocked his path.

"We're playing mini-golf because it's fun. And since you suck at pool, I figured there might be a shot of some real competition here," Carson answered with a sigh. "Jesus, Lieutenant, just putt the fucking ball up that slope and gravity will bring it down to the other side."

Will looked up with a glare he normally reserved for terrorists. "I know what to do, asshole. I'm just mentally preparing."

For fuck's sake. Carson crossed his arms and waited. Impatiently. They were only on the fourth hole of this shitty nine-hole course and they'd been here for an hour already, all because Will Charleston had to mentally prepare every freaking time he putted.

Two minutes later, Will tapped the ball. It rolled up the little brown mountain slope, lost momentum, and rolled right back to his feet.

"Shit!" the lieutenant roared. "I swear, this course is defective."

Carson couldn't help it. He laughed. Really hard. And when his stomach started to hurt, he bent over and wheezed for a couple of seconds. After he'd recovered, he glanced up to see Will hopping over the three-foot mountain with the ball in his hand.

Carson walked around to the side just as Will was setting the ball down a foot from the hole. "Hey, no cheating," he objected, wiping tears of laughter from the corners of his eyes.

"This isn't cheating. It's effective problem solving. Got a problem with that, Ensign?"

Carson rolled his eyes. Will always resorted to calling him by his lower rank when he was feeling cranky. Ah well. Carson wasn't one to judge—God knows he was feeling pretty cranky himself.

Fine, not cranky. More like ridiculously sexually frustrated.

He still felt like kicking himself for not taking Holly up on her offer Friday night. For passing up on what was guaranteed to be some more spectacular sex. But he'd had no choice. He'd meant what he told her— he wasn't interested in one-night stands or flings anymore. He wasn't sure if he was ready for a serious relationship either, but he was willing to give it a shot.

And maybe he was crazy, but he wanted to try it with Holly. He barely knew her, but what he did know, he totally liked. She was gorgeous. Funny. A little quirky. Even her confession that she was a good girl hadn't turned him off. Because, really, would a good girl have propositioned a stranger in a nightclub? Obviously Holly had a dark, wild side that was just begging to be explored...

Of course, if he weren't such an idiot, he could be the one exploring it with her right now.

"Finally!"

Forcing all thoughts of Holly out of his mind, Carson turned his attention to Will, who'd successfully putted his ball into the hole and was marking down his score on one of the little scorecards the kid at the main booth had given them.

It was weird hanging out with just Will. Carson had never really spent much time alone with the quiet SEAL, but since Garrett was on his honeymoon and the other guys were busy, Will had been the only one around.

"Now who's slacking?" came Will's voice.

Carson glanced down at the layout of the next hole and putted the ball into the mouth of a creepy-looking clown. It popped out the other side, an inch from the cup.

Will went next, and the clown spat the ball back out, a mechanical voice shrieking, "Try again, loser!"

And that was the end of the game.

Very calmly, Will lifted his putter and whipped it at the clown's smiling red mouth. "Never ask me to do this again," he growled as he stomped off the green.

With a sigh, Carson retrieved the putter Will had thrown and headed for the booth. After handing everything back to the kid in charge, he walked toward the chain-link fence at the entrance of the mini-putt course, where the lieutenant was lighting up a cigarette.

"Aw shit, you said you quit," Carson said, frowning with disapproval.

A pair of brown-bordering-on-black eyes glared at him. "I don't need another lecture about my bad habits." Will took a deep, defiant drag of his smoke.

"*Another* lecture? Who else was giving you grief about it?"

"A friend."

The two men left the course and strode in the direction of the gravel parking lot. It was just past three, and the sun was still high in the sky, a bright yellow canopy that made Carson squint as they walked to his Range Rover.

Next to him, Will pulled out a pair of sunglasses from the front pocket of his golf shirt and slid them on. The mirrored shades made him look like the Terminator, or maybe a badass cop. Carson always felt like a pretty boy next to the other man. He and Will both stood at six-three, but Carson's dirty-blond hair and blue eyes had never seemed as macho as Will's dark crew cut and the I'm-gonna-kick-your-ass black-eyed glare he had going on.

"A friend, huh," Carson mused. "Would that friend be Melanie?"

"Mackenzie," Will corrected, setting his square jaw. His eyes were covered, but his ragged sigh was clear confirmation that he still hadn't managed to score with the mysterious woman he'd been hung up on for years. Carson didn't know much about the situation, but some of the cryptic comments Will had made over the years led him to believe that the guy was disgustingly in love with this Mackenzie.

"So you two went to high school together, in that zero-population town you grew up in?" Carson asked, trying to pry out a few more details.

"Hunter Ridge. It's a few hours east of San Diego, and it has a population of five thousand, asshole."

Carson unlocked the Rover and opened the driver's door. Will hopped in the passenger side, immediately rolling down the window. The car had air conditioning, but Will didn't seem to care.

"So anyway, that's the girl, right? The high-school sweetheart?" Carson prompted.

He wasn't sure why he was pushing for details, but lately he'd come to realize he knew next to nothing about the other man. He and Will had been on the same SEAL team for four years now, and while Carson knew most of the other guys better than he knew his own family, Will remained a mystery. Garrett said some dudes were just like that, secretive to the death, but it didn't seem right to Carson.

"Best friend." Will's reply came out tense and strained, as if he'd rather pour hot wax over his body than say the words.

"Okay. Best friend." Carson started the car and reversed out of the parking spot. "So this best friend, what does she do, you know, for a living?"

"She makes jewelry."

"Is she any good?"

To Carson's extreme astonishment, Will let out a long, genuine laugh. "Actually, no. Her jewelry sucks. She knows it, everyone in town knows it, but people humor her because she won't accept money for—" He halted instantly.

Curiosity trickled through him. "She won't accept money for what? Oh man, is she a hooker?"

"She's not a fucking hooker," Will shot back. "Jesus."

"Then what does she do, aside from making bad jewelry?"

Silence stretched between them and Carson's curiosity transformed into a spark of concern. Maybe this was why Will was so serious all the time. Maybe he was hung up on some nut job.

"She's a psychic," Will finally admitted. He glanced over at Carson as if gauging his reaction.

Having never been a big believer of paranormal junk like psychics, Carson had to swallow back his incredulity. This woman was obviously important to Will, and he didn't want to step on any toes. So instead he kept his eyes on the road and said, "Is she the real thing?"

"Unfortunately. So what's the deal with you and the waitress from the wedding?" And that was it. Subject dropped. Will was very good at that, changing topics before you could blink.

Carson turned on Harbor and onto the Coronado Bay Bridge, driving in the direction of Will's house. Will was the only member of the team who lived this close to the base. All the other guys lived in San Diego. Well, except for Garrett, who'd been spending every night at Shelby's Coronado apartment ever since the two had fallen madly in love.

"There's no deal," Carson said as he came to a halt at a stop sign.

Will grinned. "She refused to go home with you, huh?"

He bristled. "Actually, I refused to go home with *her*."

"Why'd you do that?"

"Because…" Before he could stop it, the truth rolled right out of his mouth. "Because I want to date her and she just wants a fling."

Will laughed. Jeez, two laughs in the span of ten minutes. Maybe he was drunk. "Since when do you date?"

"Since now."

The other man nodded wisely. "Ah, so you realized it's time to grow up."

"Something like that."

"And you like this girl?"

"From what I know so far, yeah," he admitted.

Will gave a careless shrug. "Then have sex with her."

"Did you not just hear a word I said?" Carson said in frustration.

"Sure I did. But the way I see it, it's your in. Call her up, tell her you're up for a fling, and then slowly work on her to try the dating thing."

"She was pretty determined to do the fling thing, man."

"Then change her mind. You're a SEAL, she's a cute little waif. How hard could it be?"

Carson paused. Will did have a point. He wanted Holly, and he wasn't going to get her standing around playing mini-golf. Maybe he *should* call her. Agree to sleep together for a while, and then turn up the seductive charm and convince her to give him a serious shot…

"Definitely an idea worth considering," he finally admitted, pulling up in front of Will's small, non-descript bungalow. He put the car in park and turned to the other man. "Well, I'd like to say thanks for a good game of golf, but I can't. Why? Because you hurled your putter at a clown and threw a hissy fit."

"I didn't throw a hissy fit. I was only displaying my dislike for that sad excuse of a course. Next time you want to play mini-golf, call a third-grader. I only play adult golf."

"Adult golf? So you play naked while someone films you? Thanks, but I'll pass."

Will gave him the finger and got out of the car.

Holly didn't get home from the Grier wedding until past midnight, after spending the entire night serving drinks and fighting off the advances of the very drunk uncle of the bride. Her temples were throbbing as she got out of her bright yellow VW Beetle and headed up the flower-lined path leading to her building.

Shoving her hand in her black leather purse, she fiddled around for her keys, found them and stepped toward the lobby door.

"You're home late," a male voice drawled.

She jumped, searching the darkness. She finally spotted him leaning against one of the pillars near the entrance.

"What on earth are you doing here?" she demanded.

Carson shot her a charming grin. "You're not in the least bit happy to see me?"

Happy? Try overjoyed. Just the sight of him, in faded blue jeans that hugged his muscular legs and a blue sweatshirt the same color as his eyes, made her pulse race. She'd been thinking about him ever since the wedding, hoping he'd call. She couldn't even count how many times she'd stared at the phone last night, willing it to ring, but it hadn't, and she'd forced herself to accept that Carson had meant what he said. He wasn't interested in having sex with her again.

But obviously he'd changed his mind.

"How did you know where I live?"

He shrugged. "Called the catering company and told the woman who answered that I'd found your cell phone and wanted to return it."

"And she gave you my address? What if you were a serial killer?"

There was a twinkle in those ocean-blue eyes. "Do you really want to stand out here and talk about your company's irresponsible receptionist, or are you going to invite me up?"

Her pulse took off in a gallop. "You want to come up? I thought you didn't do this kind of thing anymore."

"I had a change of heart." He slanted his head. "Unless the offer's off the table…"

Holly grinned. "Oh, the offer is definitely still on the table."

"Good." He grinned back. "So why are we still out here?"

With a laugh, she unlocked the door to the lobby. Her apartment was on the second floor, but the elevator ride seemed to take hours. Carson edged close to her, sliding his hand down to fondle her ass while he bent his head and lightly nibbled her earlobe. She bit back a moan, enjoying the way he squeezed her cheeks and then dragged his finger up and down her crease. God, she couldn't wait to get naked with this man.

Finally the elevator doors opened. Impatiently, she pushed forward and practically sprinted to her door, unlocking it with shaky fingers.

Carson stood behind her as she fumbled with the handle, chuckling as she struggled, then giving her ass a quick spank when she finally got the door open. The apartment was dark when they walked in, but Holly made no move to turn on the lights.

Instead, she grabbed his hand and started to lead him toward the hallway. "Bedroom," she choked out.

"Someone's a little eager," he teased.

"A little? Try a lot. I've been fantasizing about being with you again for an entire month."

"Fantasizing, huh?" His lips were suddenly on her neck, kissing the sensitive skin, sucking it gently. "Did you lie in bed at night and touch yourself while thinking about me?"

"Yes."

He groaned against her skin. "That's hot."

"I'm glad you approve." She shuddered when his teeth nipped at her jaw. "Can we go the bedroom now?"

"It's too far away," he said huskily, then pulled her toward him and captured her mouth with his.

She didn't know how long they stood there kissing. And she definitely had no idea how they ended up in the kitchen, the closest room to the front hall. But suddenly they were there, and Carson had dragged her toward the small island in the center of the room.

His rough hands gripped her ass and then he was lifting her up onto the counter.

"Ever done it on this counter?" he drawled, stepping closer and toying with the side zipper of her black skirt.

"Can't say I have."

Her thighs shook when she saw him lick his lips. Oh God. He looked about ready to devour her. "Can I be honest?" he asked.

"Are you ever anything but?"

"No, not really." He smiled wolfishly. "And right now I honestly need to tell you that I've been dying to lick your pussy since the moment I met you."

A jolt of arousal thudded between her legs. Lord, if he kept talking like that, she'd probably end up coming before he even touched her.

With a grin, he unzipped her skirt and slowly peeled the material down her legs, leaving her in a pair of white bikini panties. His grin widened when he saw the damp spot on her underwear, indisputable evidence that she was extremely turned on.

He dragged his index finger along the crotch of her panties, brushing over her swollen sex, and she experienced a burst of pleasure. "S-stop," she managed to squeeze out, and his finger froze.

"You okay?" he murmured.

She squeezed her eyes shut. "No. I'm seriously seconds away from coming, Carson."

He burst out laughing. "And that's a bad thing?" Without waiting for a response, he stuck his fingers under the waistband of her panties, lifted her ass and shoved the underwear down.

"I want it to last," she protested.

Another chuckle slid out of his throat. "Don't worry, I'll go slow. Now be a good girl and spread your legs for me, Holly."

She swallowed. Then spread.

The heat of his gaze slammed into her and pulsed through her body. He stared at her exposed pussy with piercing blue eyes, his gaze roaming over every hot, damp inch.

A rush of vulnerability welled up inside her. She almost closed her legs, wanting to stop the moisture that seeped between them, wanting to put an end to the crazy shockwaves of arousal that made her clit throb. But she didn't close her legs. No. Because Carson stepped toward her again, and he was licking his lips again, and his eyes glittered with raw, unadulterated lust, and…oh God, he was touching her.

He moved his finger along her folds, up and down, the gentle, teasing caress nearly causing her to topple off the counter. "Tell me what you like," he said roughly.

"I like everything you're doing so far."

Sliding over her clit, he rubbed the swollen nub for a few moments before moving lower and toying with her wet opening with the tip of his finger. "And this?" he prompted.

"Also good," she croaked.

Before she could blink, that talented finger pushed into her, deep inside, drawing a moan from her throat.

Carson grinned, and then she blinked again and he wasn't looming over her anymore. He'd sunk to his knees, his finger still buried inside her, his gorgeous mouth now inches from her thighs.

"So," he said thoughtfully. He moved his finger in and out, a slow torturous rhythm that had her squirming on the counter. "How close *are* you?"

"Um, really close."

"Yeah? So if I put my tongue *here*…" she gasped as he lightly flicked his tongue over her clit, "…you'll explode?"

"Any fucking second," she said hoarsely.

He laughed again, and Holly felt a flicker of annoyance at his amusement over his situation. Didn't he realize she wasn't kidding? Little flutters of orgasm were already floating through her body, waiting to crash to the surface, her clit ached so badly it hurt, and he was *laughing* at her.

She opened her mouth. "It's really not fun—"

He withdrew his finger and replaced it with his tongue.

She closed her mouth.

Pleasure swarmed her body. Carson's beard stubble scraped against her hyper-sensitized thighs, his mouth hot and eager as he pressed it to her aching pussy. And his tongue…oh lord. His tongue lapped her up in long sensual strokes that stoked the fire in her belly and made her toes curl and—yup, she was going to come.

Holly bit her lip, closed her eyes, and desperately tried to tamp down the rising orgasm. But his mouth felt so good and…*oh yes!*

The orgasm ripped through her, stealing the breath right out of her lungs while shards of bright light distorted her vision. She gave a desperate moan, pressed her hands to Carson's head and brought him closer, milking all the pleasure she could

When the agonizing ecstasy finally abated, she opened her eyes to find Carson grinning at her again. He wiped his chin and gave a small chuckle. "Um, okay, so you weren't bluffing," he said ruefully.

"I told you." She cleared her throat when she heard how husky her voice sounded. "I couldn't help it...it was...too good."

"Don't apologize for coming, sweetheart."

She started to shift off the counter, but he quickly reached up with two large hands and kept her in place. "And don't even think about getting up. That orgasm was just to take the edge off. Now I can *really* get started."

Huh? Before she could ask what his definition of getting started was, he'd already pressed his lips back to her clit.

"Carson, you already—" Her voice died in her throat as he swirled his tongue over her.

Okay, so this man was obviously more than just a skilled soldier. As his mouth worked its magic on her again, Holly decided Carson Scott was her new hero. She also decided she would be a complete moron if she argued with him about this.

So she simply leaned back on her elbows, closed her eyes and lost herself in his sexual ministrations.

"You taste like heaven, sweetheart." He slid his tongue over her pussy and groaned. "I could stay here for the rest of my life and never get bored with this sweet cunt of yours."

She added *extremely good dirty talker* to the growing list of *Things Carson Excels At.*

Another moan slipped out when he suckled her clit between his warm lips. Her entire body throbbed with restless arousal, as if the orgasm he'd just given it wasn't enough. And no, it wasn't enough. She wanted more.

Her nipples pebbled against her bra, demanding some attention of their own. She reached up to touch her breasts, then lowered her hands, feeling embarrassed.

Carson lifted his head and rolled his eyes. "I saw that. Now bring those hands right back to those gorgeous tits of yours and make yourself feel good."

"Do it for me," she taunted with a tiny smile.

"I'm busy." And then his head dipped between her thighs again and his mouth resumed feasting.

Shockwaves of pleasure rocketed through her. His tongue flicked over her clit with just enough pressure that she could feel the faint quivers of another orgasm. Her hands trembled as she reached for her breasts again, but this time there was no hesitation. So what if she fondled her own boobs? Carson obviously enjoyed it.

She pulled her shirt over her head and unclasped her bra, tossing both garments aside. Her nipples were painfully hard when she touched them. She'd always had sensitive breasts, but Steve never gave them the attention they craved. She wanted Carson's tongue on them, wanted him to suck each rigid bud deep in his mouth, to lick her and bite her and make her scream with pleasure. But like he said, he was busy, and she was definitely enjoying his other task.

He sucked on her clit again and then shoved two long fingers inside her. She was so wet she could feel her wetness trickling down her thighs. How was that possible? She and Steve had always needed a tube of lubrication when they'd had sex.

Don't think about Steve.

Right. She seriously needed to quit comparing her ex to the man between her legs.

Not that there was even a comparison to be made.

"Are you going to come for me again?" Carson muttered, adding a third finger into the mix.

She whimpered and managed a strained, "Yes." Then she pinched her nipples and the whimper became a moan. She was close. Pleasure built up inside her. All it would take was one more stroke of his tongue, one more thrust of his fingers…

Carson pressed his fingers hard against her G-spot, sucked harder on her clit, and she exploded.

The climax was just as intense as the first, just as fierce and all-consuming, and this one didn't end. It just roared on, rippling through her body while bursts of bliss sparked her nerve endings.

"Carson," she moaned, fighting for breath. "It's too much…it's…"

Rather than release her, he continued to tongue her, his fingers sliding in and out with long, deep thrusts until she was coming again. Or maybe she'd never stopped coming the first time. Who knew. Who cared. Holly's pulse shrieked in her ears, her breasts throbbed beneath her trembling fingers. And the pleasure…it never ended. The dam had broken and a rush of pure ecstasy poured through her in waves.

"Oh yeah," Carson groaned, lifting his head after planting one last soft kiss to her clit.

She gasped for air, her body so sated and numb she couldn't move a single limb or muscle.

He rose to his feet and pushed her hands off her breasts, quickly replacing them with his own. His palms cupped each mound, his fingers stroking. Bending his head, he tasted her, covering one nipple with his mouth and sucking gently. He groaned again, then moved away from her breast and captured her lips in a hot kiss.

She kissed him back eagerly, enjoying the warmth of his mouth, the taste of herself on his tongue. Lifting her arms, she twined them around his strong, corded neck and pulled him closer, needing to feel his rock-hard body pressed against her. He stepped closer and she widened her legs, allowing him to push his jean-clad lower body into the junction of her thighs.

"You're so hard," she whispered into his mouth, rubbing herself against the long erection bulging at his crotch. The denim scraped over her naked sex, but the slight abrasion only turned her on even more.

"Hold on a second," he choked out. "All that rubbing is too distracting."

She quit moving and waited for him to grab a condom from his pocket. Shoving his jeans down, he sheathed his cock and offered a faint smile. "Okay, do your worst. Or best, actually."

Holly circled his heavy erection with her fingers and guided him to her opening. They released simultaneous moans as he slid his entire length into her wetness. The feel of him inside her was so good she almost fell off the counter, but Carson grabbed her hips and steadied her, thrusting a couple of times before letting out another groan.

"Damn. I won't last long," he rasped.

"Then come. You know, to take the edge off," she said, mimicking his earlier words. "But next time, I expect at least a full hour of serious thrusting and pumping to make up for this debacle."

Laughing, he bent down to kiss her, then set out in a fast, hard pace that had her gasping against his lips. He pounded into her, all the way to the hilt, and each stroke brought her closer and closer to the edge again. When she heard Carson's low groan of pleasure, she let herself go, squeezing her inner muscles against him as his cock pulsed with release inside her.

When the waves of orgasm finally subsided, she found Carson watching her with something that resembled awe.

"What?" she asked self-consciously.

He shook his head, looking a bit stunned. "How are we this good together? The only time I've ever come this hard is when we did it in that closet."

She managed a small laugh. "Are you just trying to be nice?"

He snorted. "I just fucked you on your kitchen counter. Does a nice guy really do that?"

"Hmmm, I guess not." She tilted her head. "So…just to clarify…are you officially agreeing to fling with me?"

"I guess I am."

Wariness crept up her body. "Because I meant what I said on Friday—I don't really have the time for a relationship right now."

"Okay."

"Okay?"

He rolled his eyes. "Yes, okay. If you want sex, I'll give you sex."

"*Just* sex," she prompted.

An indefinable expression flickered in his eyes, and then he smiled. "Whatever you say, sweetheart."

Chapter Four

"YOUR PLAN ISN'T WORKING." CARSON SANK INTO THE CHAIR ACROSS from Will and handed the man a beer.

It was Monday night and he'd dragged Will to the Sand Hole, one of his favorite bars in San Diego. A few yards from the pier, the bar offered an outdoor patio that overlooked the ocean, and the two men sat at a table by the railing while the balmy evening breeze tried to claim the napkins on the tabletop. Carson finally set his beer bottle on the napkins so the damn things would quit fluttering around.

It was just Will and him tonight, something that was becoming a habit. Garrett and Shelby were still away. Ryan and Matt had hit a nightclub across town, but Carson hadn't felt like clubbing tonight. He was in a seriously shitty mood, despite the incredible sex he'd been having for the past week.

"She still wants a fling, huh?" Will said, slowly sipping his beer.

"Yep." Carson groaned. "Don't get me wrong—the fucking is unbelievable. But every time I even bring up the subject of going out to dinner or catching a movie, she tries to distract me with sex."

Will laughed. "Does it work?"

"Every fucking time, man." He was almost ashamed of how badly he craved Holly's lithe little body. Every time she was naked, he couldn't think. Or breathe. Or do anything that didn't involve running his tongue over every inch of her nakedness.

It was like an addiction, and one he could spend the rest of his life enslaved to. But that was the problem—he wasn't going to have Holly for the rest of his life. Hell, if she had her way, he wouldn't have her for much longer.

"She's got midterm exams coming up, and she keeps hinting that we need to take a breather," he confessed with a sigh.

"Culinary school has exams?"

"Kind of. She's got to prepare all these fancy dishes for her teacher, and then work in a restaurant for a couple of nights to show she's capable of working under pressure and all that crap."

"Bring her on our next assignment." Will snorted. "She'll definitely learn how to work under pressure then."

Carson lifted his beer to his lips, suddenly sidetracked. "Speaking of assignments, what's this I've been hearing about us going to the jungle?" The idea of hopping in a chopper and going somewhere—even the freaking jungle—wasn't all that unappealing. The team hadn't been out of the country since that stint in Colombia, and Carson was itching for an adventure. He hated sitting around and waiting to be paged.

"Not for sure yet," Will replied. "But I've been hearing rumors about some trouble happening at a plant in Brazil. Rebel soldiers killed a few workers, I think, and there's a chance we might need to go in and extract the CEO. He refuses to leave, but there've been a few threats to his life, so we'll see." Will put down his beer. "You're feeling stir crazy too, eh? Thought you were too busy wooing the waitress to remember what you do for a living."

"Well, maybe the best way to change her mind is to leave," he said with a shrug. "You know, absence makes the heart grow fonder, and all that? I swear, she's got so much shit on her plate, I'm starting to think she's Superwoman."

Will looked curious. "Yeah? Like what?"

"Work, this culinary class, and don't get me started on her incompetent family. I can't count how many times she's left me in her bed this week so she could rush off and save someone from themselves." Carson shook his head, baffled. "Her father calls her to come over and help him check his email! And her sister Caroline is a total space cadet. She locked her keys in the car every day this week."

And when they said jump, Holly jumped. That's what Carson didn't get. His sister Jenny was constantly getting into jams, but she only called Carson when something bad was going down. Holly's family, however, called for everything. Every goddamn miniscule problem that they could probably handle all on their own, if Holly would just let them.

He knew her mother had died, and that sucked, but he didn't think it was reason enough for Holly to drop everything and play mother hen to everyone. Especially when all the responsibilities—which she could easily rid herself of—constantly got in the way of their relationship.

Sorry, their *fling*. Because no matter how much fun they had together, how many times they laughed over pizza or cuddled in front of the television or had wild sex on every surface of Holly's apartment, she still refused to call it anything other than a fling.

"So tell her how ridiculous her family is being," Will suggested.

"I've tried. But she thinks they need her. The whole family was pretty upset after her mother died, and Holly ended up filling her mom's role. Now they all expect it of her."

Will leaned back in his chair. "Do you like this girl?"

Did he like her? Uh, yeah. In fact, he couldn't remember ever liking another female more than he liked Holly. She was quirky and funny and unbelievably good in bed. And way too caring and generous for her own good.

"Of course I like her," he answered.

"Then tell her. And keep telling her. Sooner or later she'll have to see that the two of you could have more than a silly fling."

But would she? Carson had the most unsettling feeling that it wouldn't matter how many times he told her how great she was, or how many ways he tried to show her he was serious about her. With Holly, responsibility always came first. To her job, her family, her school.

So that meant he had to find a way around it. Because he was sick of being Holly Lawson's boy toy. He wanted to be her boyfriend.

Now he just had to convince her to let him.

"WANT A SLICE OF PIZZA?" CARSON ASKED AFTER HE'D GOTTEN RID OF the condom, leaving her in a hot, sweaty mess on the living room carpet.

Holly forced her head up to shoot him an amazed look. How was he even able to stand up? Her own legs were so shaky she knew she'd keel right over if she tried putting her weight on them. She was nowhere close to Carson's level of recovery.

"Sex makes me hungry," he said with an endearing shrug.

She managed to move into a sitting position, watching as Carson flipped open the pizza box, grabbed a slice and sank down on the couch. Naked. The sight of that gloriously nude body stole the breath right out of her lungs. She'd never seen a man in such incredible shape before. Carson's chest was solid and unyielding, defined pecs and rippled six-pack and smooth sleek sinew. A dusting of blond hair covered his chest and legs, but it was just the right amount. Not too hairy, and not pretty-boy smooth. He was masculine and beautiful and so appealing, her mouth watered like one of Pavlov's dogs.

He cast her a grin when he noticed her staring, then gestured to the cushion next to his. "Sit and eat."

Somehow she managed to force her legs to carry her from the floor to the couch. She grabbed a slice of pizza, but she wasn't all that hungry; she just wanted to hold something in her hands so she wouldn't be tempted to grab Carson. Boy, was she tempted. The aftereffects of her orgasm still pulsated through her body, tingling her nipples, tickling her thighs. She'd never experienced anything like this. The primitive, animal lust and raw pleasure.

It had been like this for an entire week. She couldn't keep her hands off this man, and if it weren't for work and school, she would be content being with him from morning 'til night and doing nothing but having really amazing sex.

Knowing Carson, he'd be totally up for the idea. He'd spent every night at her place for the past week, and he didn't seem at all bored with her yet. Which was odd, since she really wasn't the most exciting person on the planet. When she was at her apartment—and not rescuing her siblings from themselves—she usually spent her time cooking or watching TV. Not exactly anything to write home about.

Yet Carson seemed perfectly at ease doing nothing with her. Tonight he'd even brought over a couple of DVDs, all action flicks. They'd watched one before taking a break to have sex on the living room floor, and he'd spent the entire movie scrutinizing the fake military troop and telling Holly all the reasons why they wouldn't have been able to blow up the village using the equipment they had. His commentary had reminded her of what he did for a living, that his job was a dangerous one, but it still didn't seem real to her, especially since he seemed to spend most of his time waiting to be paged.

"Aren't you bored not blowing up things or traipsing through the jungle?" she found herself asking, setting her pizza slice back in the box.

Next to her, Carson chewed slowly, then tossed her a thoughtful look. "Yes and no. The team hasn't gone wheels up in more than a month, and I'm definitely ready for another assignment. But I'm also enjoying spending time with you, so I'm not complaining about the lull in the SEAL world."

"We're not spending time together," she reminded him. "We're sleeping together."

As if her reminder had stolen his appetite, he dropped his half-eaten slice. "Right," he said, sounding a bit sarcastic.

"It's a fling, Carson," she said firmly.

"Not anymore it isn't." He raked his fingers through his blond hair. "We've spent a week together, Hol. We've cuddled and watched movies and made each other laugh. That's more than a fling, in my opinion."

She pressed her lips together, trying to think of a response. He was right—they had done a lot of couple-ish things this week. But they'd had a ridiculous amount of sex, too, so she'd figured that canceled out the couple stuff. Not that she didn't enjoy the non-sex parts. She did enjoy them. She was just…

Scared, a little voice filled in.

Holly quickly forced away the thought. No, she wasn't scared. She couldn't be. So what if Steve had dumped her and told her he wanted someone more wild and exciting? That wasn't the reason she didn't want a relationship. She was simply too busy for one.

Liar. You're scared.

The voice was beginning to annoy her. In fact, this whole conversation with Carson was beginning to annoy her. Why couldn't he stop pushing her and just have fun? The two of them had become pretty skilled at *fun*.

Obviously it was time to remind him of that.

Before he could open his mouth to continue speaking, she slid closer and wrapped her fingers around his shaft. It instantly hardened against her palm.

"Oh no you don't," he grumbled, reaching for her hand. "You're not going to distract me again. We're having this conversation whether you like it or—Jesus," he groaned as she bent down and took his tip into her mouth.

Kissing the broad head, she trailed her tongue along his sensitive underside, nibbling gently on the velvety smooth flesh.

"Damn it, Holly. You're not allowed to…" His voice trailed off the moment she sucked him.

There was nothing more arousing than bringing Carson to climax. She'd done it frequently this week, and she knew exactly what he liked now. Curling her fingers around his base, she pumped and sucked his shaft, swirling her tongue over the tip on each upstroke. His husky moans and the way he lifted his hips to thrust deeper into her mouth told her she'd succeeded in distracting him again.

His cock throbbed against her tongue and his hands tangled in her hair, signaling he was close. "Can I come in your mouth?" he rasped.

She nodded, chuckling against his hard male flesh. He asked her that every time she did this, but she didn't mind. She liked that he cared enough to ask.

With a ragged groan, he let himself go. Holly swallowed every drop, gently kneading his balls as he shuddered with release. When she looked up, she saw his blue eyes were glazed, swimming with sated desire.

"You're evil," he squeezed out, falling back against the sofa cushions and pulling her naked body on top of his. "You've got to stop doing that."

She blinked innocently. "I thought you liked my blowjobs."

"I love your blowjobs, sweetheart, and you know it. But you can't keep avoiding—" Before he could finish, the phone on the coffee table began to buzz.

Carson sat up with irritation and shot her a warning look. "Don't even think about it, Holly."

She got off his lap and started to reach for the phone. "I can't not answer. What if it's someone in my family? Or work?"

"That's exactly why you shouldn't answer it," he muttered.

Ignoring him, she clicked the *talk* button and pressed the phone to her ear. "Hello?"

"Holly, I have an emergency," came her sister Caroline's desperate voice.

A lump of resentment lodged in her throat. "What is it, Caroline?"

Her sister didn't get a chance to explain, because Carson had grabbed the phone from Holly's hands. She let out a yelp of protest, but he was already speaking.

"Caroline?" He swatted Holly's hands away when she tried to swipe the phone back. "I'm Carson...Holly's boyfriend."

"What are you doing?" Holly hissed.

He paused. "I know she didn't mention it. It's still fairly new...uh-huh....yup. So, what seems to be the problem, Caroline?"

Holly swallowed down her anger as she watched Carson listen to her sister's response. How dare he? He had no right acting like a jerk and taking the phone from her like this.

"Really?" He nodded to himself. "Well, here's what you're going to do, sweetheart. You're going to knock on your super's door and ask him to let him into your apartment." He paused again. "No, Holly doesn't need to be there for that. She's very busy right now."

Holly fumed at him, crossing her arms over her chest to cover her bare breasts.

"Well, tomorrow morning you can take a cab over here and get the spare keys you gave to Holly, and make copies of them. Your original set might turn up..." He sighed. "Then change the locks if you think someone might find them, figure out your address and let themselves into your apartment... How? A locksmith can do that for you." He shook his head again. "No, Holly cannot change your locks for you. You can't expect her to do everything for you, sweetheart... Hey, you know what, Caroline? I've got to go. Holly and I are about to watch a movie. Call back when you've gotten into your apartment, okay?" Without saying goodbye, he hung up.

On her sister!

Holly watched as he nonchalantly placed the phone on the coffee table and turned to look at her. "Ready to watch the rest of that movie?" he asked pleasantly.

She didn't answer. Anger bubbled in her stomach. "Why did you do that?" she demanded.

He shrugged. "Because I'm sick of watching your sexy ass slide through the front door every time one of them calls you up for help."

"This isn't your family, Carson. It's mine. And what I choose to do for them isn't your concern."

He blew out a frustrated breath. "She lost her apartment key, for fuck's sake. It's not the end of the world! And what I told her to do is what you *wouldn't* have told her if you'd taken that call. You would've hopped in your car and taken care of everything for her."

"So?" she said defensively.

"So, it's not your freaking job, sweetheart." He looked exasperated. "Caroline is five years older—she should be taking care of *you*, not the other way around. She takes advantage of you. They all do."

Discomfort filled her body. Although a part of her knew he was right—the part that had been feeling the same way for two years now—she still couldn't let go of her anger. So what if her family took advantage of her? They were still *her* family. Not his. And trying to stop her from taking care of them was presumptuous and selfish of him. This was Steve all over again, making demands, telling her to forget about everyone and everything else in her life and just focus on him. Well, she couldn't do that.

"You shouldn't have interfered," she said coolly.

Carson dragged one hand through his hair, frazzled. "I won't apologize for it. It's time you quit focusing all your energy on them."

"And do what, focus it all on *you*?"

Before he could answer, she stumbled to her feet, suddenly very aware that they'd been conducting this entire argument while naked. Whirling around, she stomped down the hall to the bedroom, where she threw some clothes on.

"Come on, Holly, don't be mad," came his low voice from the doorway. "I was only trying to help."

"By hanging up on my sister? That was unbelievably rude of you." She turned to face him, glad he'd put on his jeans so she couldn't get distracted by his gorgeous body. "I'm not happy with you right now, Carson. And…" She took a breath. "I want you to leave."

His blue eyes darkened. "You don't mean that."

"Yeah, I do." She clenched her jaw. "Isn't that what you wanted? Me being honest with the people in my life? Well, I'm being honest. I'm too pissed off to have this fight right now, so I want you to leave."

His mouth tightened in a thin line. "Fine. You want me to go, I'll go." He turned, then shot her a glance over his shoulder. "But this isn't over, Holly. Maybe I stepped over a line tonight, but I did it for you. You spend so much time worrying about your family that you never have enough time for yourself. I just wanted you to have one night that's only about *you*, not them. Because I care about you, and I want..." He let out a slow breath. "I want to be with you, and I know you want to be with me."

Her heart ached as a sad expression filled his face.

"And, baby, we'd both be a lot better off if you'd just admit it." With that, he slid out the door.

Chapter Five

OKAY, SO SHE WAS AN IDIOT. IT TOOK HOLLY ONLY TWENTY-FOUR HOURS to figure it out, though a part of her had known all along she was being foolish by keeping Carson at arm's length. Ever since the night she'd met him at the Hot Zone, she'd felt more alive, more *free*, than she had in years. Instead of holding on to that feeling, she'd sent Carson away, and now she felt more trapped than ever.

Then again, was it possible to feel anything other than trapped when she was having dinner with her family?

"Pass the mashed potatoes," Todd said through a mouthful of sesame chicken Holly had prepared.

She obediently passed him the bowl of potatoes, then glanced around the table at the rest of them. Her father's dark head was bent as he cut his chicken, her brother Kyle was slathering butter on the rolls Holly had spent the past two hours baking, and Caroline was pushing peas around her plate with her fork, looking distracted.

And had any of them commented on her dinner? Nope. Even though Caroline had called her at the last minute, Holly had run around her kitchen, cooking, packing everything up so she could bring it over to her dad's house for this unexpected dinner *Caroline* had planned. Instead of working on the recipes she was creating for her midterms, she'd slaved to make this stupid meal, and none of them had even thanked her for it.

It only made her realize that Carson had been absolutely right when he'd told her they took advantage of her. She'd always known it, but hearing someone else say it had forced her to really examine the situation. And she didn't like what she saw. Ever since her mom died, she'd done everything for her family.

When was the last time any of them had thanked her for it?

"I have my last exam tomorrow," Todd spoke up, taking a sip of water. "Hol, do you think you could come over to my dorm after dinner tonight and quiz me?"

Her lips automatically formed the word *yes* but she quickly snapped her mouth closed. No. *No.* So what if it was Todd's final exam? She had *her* evaluation next week, and if she wanted to impress her teacher, she needed to come up with a recipe that would knock the man's socks off. Wasn't that more important?

If Carson were here, she knew he'd say yes, it *was* more important, and a sudden flare of determination lit up inside her.

"I can't," she told her brother. "I have my own exam to prepare for."

Todd looked startled. "You can't? But it'll only take a few hours. Please, Holly?"

She was about to firmly reject him again, when her older sister suddenly slammed a hand down on the table, causing the silverware to jingle loudly. Everyone turned to Caroline in surprise, even their dad, who hadn't said a word during the entire meal.

"Quit bothering Holly," Caroline said to Todd, her green eyes flashing with anger. "She said no."

Todd swallowed. "I wasn't—"

"You were being an asshole, expecting her to drop everything to help you study for an exam that you should have started reviewing for weeks ago," Caroline snapped. Her cheeks flushed. "Actually, we were *all* being assholes to Holly. Even you, Daddy."

Their father frowned.

"I'm serious," Caroline insisted. "I know we've all had a tough couple years, but yesterday I realized how unfair we've been to Holly. We expect her to do everything."

"Because she's so good at it," Kyle offered. His expression grew pained. "You know, the way Mom was."

"Yeah, but she's not Mom," Caroline retorted. "And she shouldn't have to do whatever we ask her. Did you guys know she has a boyfriend?"

The three males glanced at Holly in surprise.

She suddenly felt uncomfortable, not to mention confused. What on earth had gotten into Caroline? For two years her sister hadn't seemed to have any qualms about asking Holly for every favor imaginable—what the hell had changed?

"That's right," Caroline said, shaking her head. "She's got a boyfriend, and none of us even knew about him."

"Caroline," Holly began, wanting to say that Carson wasn't exactly her boyfriend.

Her sister silenced her with a sharp look. "No, don't explain. You have a boyfriend, and you didn't tell us, but that's not the issue. The issue is that none of us even cared to ask if you were seeing anyone new. We're jerks, Hol. We expect you to fix everything in our lives and don't bother being interested in yours. All we do is make demands. It's no wonder you got your boyfriend to hang up on me. I deserved it."

A short silence fell over the table.

Holly's father finally cleared his throat and shot her a gentle look. "Honey…is it true? Do you think we make too many demands of you?"

Holly swallowed. "Sometimes."

Her dad looked away, but not before she saw a flash of guilt in his eyes. "I'm sorry," he said. "You always seemed so eager to help out, doing all the stuff around the house that your mom used to do…" Sorrow creased his features. "And I was too busy missing your mother to notice how unfair I was being to you."

"It's okay, Daddy," she said, her voice coming out shaky.

"No, it's not. Caroline's right. Your mother's gone, and it's time we figured out how to take care of ourselves." He suddenly straightened his shoulders, his stern expression reminding her of the way he'd been before her mom had died. Strong, commanding. "First things first, I want you go home."

She faltered. "What?"

"You said you have an exam to prepare for. Go home and focus on that, honey. And while you're taking care of yourself, the rest of us are going to clean up and do the dishes and figure out exactly how we're going to make it up to you. Got it?"

She couldn't help but smile. "Got it."

She was still smiling as she left her father's house and headed for her car. Although she was a bit stunned over what just happened, she wasn't about to complain. For some reason, her family had come to their senses tonight.

No, not for some reason.

Because of Carson.

Carson had gotten through to Caroline last night. Instead of letting Holly go clean up another one of her sister's messes, he'd forced Caroline to deal with it herself. And the tough-love approach had worked. Holly had been babying them all for so long, and thanks to Carson, she wouldn't be doing that any longer. How could she have ever thought he was selfish?

I know you want to be with me…we'd both be a lot better off if you'd just admit it.

The memory of his parting words made her heart squeeze, reminding her again of just how much of a moron she was. He was right. She *did* want to be with him. She'd walked away from him that first night at the club because she'd been scared of the intense desire he'd evoked inside her. And she'd walked away from him yesterday because that intense desire had transformed into something a little too close to love, and that had scared her more.

But she wasn't scared anymore. Steve might have broken her heart, but Carson had put the pieces back together.

So maybe it was time to stop acting like an idiot and give him what he wanted. What *she* wanted.

Starting the car, Holly reversed out of the driveway, knowing exactly what she needed to do.

CARSON WASN'T PICKING UP HIS PHONE. HOLLY LEFT HIM THREE VOICE mails, but by the next day, he still hadn't called back. She would have driven over to his apartment, but she was ashamed that she didn't even know where he lived. She'd tried so hard to keep him at a distance, to keep things on her own turf, that she hadn't bothered to find out his address.

By the time early evening rolled around, she was getting frustrated. She needed to see him, damn it. Apologize for calling him selfish and asking him to leave, when all he'd tried to do was show her that it was time to stop letting her family take advantage of her.

There was only one other way she could think to find him, so just after six, she got into her car and drove across the bridge to Coronado. At John and Shelby Garrett's wedding, she'd overheard that the bride ran a bakery and coffee shop near the Navy base, so Holly headed in that direction. She found the place quickly—the name, Shelby's Bakery Café, helped narrow it down—and parked at the curb out front.

The bell over the door chimed as she stepped inside. A few elderly women sat at a small table by the window, sipping coffee, but the gorgeous blonde from the wedding was nowhere in sight. Holly drifted through the doorway that separated the café from the bakery, and found Shelby Garrett standing behind the counter, blowing her nose with a crumpled tissue.

It was obvious the other woman was upset, and Holly was about to back away when Shelby caught sight of her.

With a strained smile, Shelby said, "Can I help you?"

"You're Shelby, right?"

The blonde nodded.

Holly offered a smile of her own. "I'm Holly Lawson. I work for the company that catered your wedding."

A spark of recognition filled Shelby's blue eyes. Holly couldn't help but notice how pretty the woman was. Shelby looked like she belonged in an advertisement for surfing gear or something, all California girl good looks.

"Is this about the check we wrote?" Shelby asked with a sigh. "Johnny swore he put the right date on it, but he accidentally postdate his checks all the time."

"No, as far as I know, everything is fine." Holly moved closer to the counter, pretending not to notice the other woman's red-rimmed eyes and blotchy cheeks. She hoped there wasn't trouble in paradise already. The couple she'd seen at the wedding had looked so disgustingly in love, it would be a shame if they'd somehow lost that lovin' feeling.

"I'm actually here about something else. Well, some*one*." She swallowed, absently glancing at the cakes in the refrigerated glass cases next to the counter. "Carson Scott. He's your husband's friend, right?"

A rosy blush swept over Shelby's cheeks. "A friend of both of ours, actually."

Holly could sense there was a whole story behind that one sentence, but this probably wasn't the best time to pry. Instead, she moistened her lips and said, "I'm trying to get in touch with him but he's not answering his phone. I was hoping maybe you could give me his address." She quickly pressed on. "I swear, I'm not a crazy stalker or anything. Carson and I...have been seeing each other, I guess. I just needed to talk to him."

"I'm afraid his address isn't going to help you right now. The team left for an assignment last night. I have no idea where they are, or when they'll be back." Shelby had barely finished her last sentence when a few tears slid down her cheeks again. Looking embarrassed, she swiped at them with the sleeve of her green V-neck shirt. "I'm sorry. I know, it's pathetic, huh? I shouldn't get this hysterical over John being away. It's what he does. I knew that when I married him." She blinked a few times, her lashes spiky with wetness. "But it still sucks, you know? Never knowing if he's okay. Making coffee and baking cakes while he's God-knows-where, possibly getting shot at."

With a shaky breath, Shelby raised her tissue and blew her nose again.

Her words brought a spark of alarm to Holly's gut. Getting shot at? She'd been so focused on herself ever since she'd met Carson that she hadn't given much thought to what the life of a SEAL was like. God, was he in danger right now? The idea sent her pulse racing.

"Shit, I scared you, didn't I?" Shelby blurted out. She tossed her tissue in the wastebasket behind her and quickly rounded the counter. "I'm sorry. I wasn't trying to freak you out."

Holly gulped. "I'm not freaked out. Though I am kinda worried now."

Shelby offered a mild smile. "Goes with the territory. Do you want a cup of coffee?"

What she wanted was to hear Carson's voice and make sure he wasn't dead, but she found herself nodding. "Sure."

The blonde poured two cups, then led Holly into the café, where they sat down. "So how long have you been seeing Carson?" Shelby asked curiously.

"A week and a half, but we met about a month ago. At your bachelorette party, actually."

Shelby's delicate brows soared. "Seriously?"

"You look surprised."

"Well, I am. Carson doesn't usually stay with one girl for long." Shelby shot her an apologetic look. "No offense to you or anything."

"None taken." Holly sipped her coffee. "He told me all about it."

Again Shelby's cheeks flushed. "He did? Damn, that's awkward, then."

Holly blinked. "It is?"

"Well, most women wouldn't enjoy having coffee with someone their boyfriend has slept with."

Holly choked mid-sip. "You slept with Carson? Does your husband know?"

The other woman laughed. "Uh, yeah, he knows. He was there."

After a beat, Holly burst out laughing, too. Figured. Carson had told her he'd led a pretty racy life, so she really wasn't surprised to find out he'd had a threesome with his best friend and best friend's now-wife. Oddly enough, she wasn't angry, or even jealous. Besides, the fact that Carson had chosen to leave his casual lifestyle for *her* was kind of flattering.

"God, I'm an idiot," Holly burst out.

Shelby laughed again. "Um, okay. Care to elaborate?"

Although she didn't know Shelby at all, Holly couldn't help but spill everything, from her first encounter with Carson to the fight they'd had two nights ago. "He was just trying to help," she finished, "and I called him selfish and kicked him out."

"Don't worry, he'll come back," Shelby assured her. "Trust me, if Carson wants a relationship with you, he'll fight for it. He never gives up. It's actually very annoying."

Holly gave a brief smile. "Let's hope he still wants a relationship when he gets back." Her smile faded, and a quivery breath left her throat. "Because if he doesn't, I'll kick myself for the rest of my life for letting him get away."

Chapter Six

Two weeks. He'd been gone for two weeks. And Holly was beginning to grow more than a little worried. She'd called Shelby every day since her visit to the café, and the other woman hadn't been able to provide her with any details. Apparently someone from the base had called Shelby to tell her John had been in radio contact and should be heading home soon, but other than that, Holly had no clue if Carson was okay. She hoped he was, because if he didn't come home in one piece, she was going to have a nervous breakdown.

At least one good thing had come from all the worrying. She'd tried so hard to distract herself that she'd ended up cooking up a storm, and she'd impressed the hell out of her teacher with her dishes. He told her he would give her a glowing recommendation letter to any restaurant she applied at, but at this point, Holly wasn't sure what she wanted to do. Shelby had told her a restaurant a block from the café was up for sale, and Holly was seriously considering getting a bank loan and taking the place over herself after she finished school.

But before she made any decisions about her future, she needed Carson to come home already. She missed him. Cooking dinner for him, watching those awful action movies, having mind-blowing sex. If he didn't come back soon, she didn't know what she'd do.

"Holly, are you listening to me?" her sister snapped, jerking her out of her thoughts.

She absently walked around her kitchen, holding the phone to her ear as she opened a few cabinets and tried to decide what she would make to eat. "Sorry, what were you saying?"

"The computer course Dad is taking," Caroline said impatiently. "He wants us to go over there this weekend so he can show us all the stuff he's learned. I know it'll be boring, but he's really excited about it."

Holly tried not to laugh. Ever since their dinner two weeks ago, her family had truly been making an effort to give her space. Todd had hired himself a tutor, Kyle hadn't locked his keys in his car once, Caroline had stopped dyeing her hair, and their father was learning how to use the computer to pay his bills online. So far, none of them had called her with any emergencies, which was a huge relief, since the only thing she was capable of concentrating on right now was Carson and when the hell he would come back to the States.

"Don't worry, I'll be there," she assured her sister.

"Good. I'll see you Saturday, then. Oh, and let me tell you about this guy I met at the Hot Zone last night. Hol, he was *soooo* cute! He—"

The phone beeped in her ear, cutting off Caroline's sentence.

Holly's heart skipped a beat. "Care, I've got to go. Someone's trying to be buzzed up."

She hung up before her sister could object and pressed the code that would open the lobby door. Then, with an excited yelp, she tossed the phone on the counter and dashed toward the front door. Carson! It had to be him.

Flinging open the door, she stepped into the hallway and glued her gaze to the elevator at the end of the hall. One second…two…three… The elevator doors swung open, and a wave of joy slammed into her. There he was, wearing khakis and a green T-shirt, his jaw covered in thick blond stubble. His blue eyes narrowed with wariness when he saw her lurking in the corridor.

He took a step forward, then stopped. "You're not gonna ask me to leave again, are you?" he called out.

"Not on your life," she called back.

A smile broke across his handsome face. "Thank fuck. Because I missed you like crazy."

With urgent strides, he crossed the hall and made his way toward her. He'd barely reached the door when she launched herself into his arms and wrapped her arms tightly around him. "I'm so glad you're okay," she murmured into the crook of his neck. "You were gone so long. I was worried."

He stroked her back with his big, warm hands and pressed a kiss to her temple. "Don't worry. We just extracted a CEO and led him through the jungle for ten days. Piece of cake."

Holly laughed, then pulled him into the apartment and closed the door behind them. "Please tell me nobody shot at you."

Carson shrugged. "There might've been a bullet or two aimed in our direction," he said vaguely.

Alarm coursed through her. "Were you hit? Are you hurt?" She immediately began running her fingers over his body in search of a hidden bandage.

Chuckling, he trapped her hands between his. "Quit doing that."

"Why?" She stared accusingly at him. "You *were* hurt!"

"No, I wasn't hurt," he replied, rolling his eyes. "But if you keep touching me I'm going to come in my pants. I've been thinking about nothing but fucking you for two weeks now, so I'm a little on edge."

A smile stretched across her mouth. "You're not allowed to come in your pants. I'm pretty sex-starved too, so don't you dare deprive me."

He smiled back, but then his expression darkened. "I didn't come here to continue the fling, sweetheart."

"Good, because I don't want to."

He faltered. "You don't?"

She reached up and pressed her palm to his chest, enjoying the sleek muscles under her fingertips. "I want more this time," she admitted, looking up to meet his eyes. "I acted like an idiot, Carson. I was scared."

"Scared," he echoed uncertainly.

"I was starting to feel something for you, and I...I guess I didn't want to deal with it. My ex dumped me because I wouldn't make him my world, and then you wanted me to tell my family to screw off, and it was too much like what Steve wanted, and..." She took a breath. "I overreacted, and I accused you of being selfish when you aren't, and I...I messed up. I'm sorry. I want nothing more than to be in a relationship with you."

Carson tilted his head, still looking unsure. "What happened to having too many responsibilities for a relationship?"

"My stress levels have lowered considerably." She quickly told him about everything that had happened with her family, and the changes in her life. "So far, they're managing just fine on their own. You were right—they needed to stand on their own two feet instead of relying on me."

"What about school?" he asked.

"I still have six months left." She shot him a grin. "But I think I'll be able to squeeze you in between classes. Don't worry, I'll make lots of time for my sexy sailor boyfriend…"

"Lots of time, huh?" His voice grew husky, while a playful glint lit his eyes. "How on earth are we going to pass the time?"

She brushed her fingers over his pecs, feeling his flat nipples harden beneath her touch. Still smiling, she moved one hand down his magnificent chest and rested it on the growing bulge at his crotch. "I'm sure we can think of something."

He groaned as she rubbed his erection, but intercepted her hand before she could reach for his zipper. "One more thing," he said gruffly. "And don't you dare try to distract me with a blowjob, because I have to say this."

She feigned annoyance. "Fine. What is it?"

"I've fallen in love with you."

The vulnerability she saw in his eyes stole the breath from her lungs. As her heart did a little somersault, she swallowed hard and said, "I'm in love with you, too."

Carson bent down and brushed his lips over hers, the gentle kiss causing her toes to curl. Then he pulled back and offered a devastating grin. "So…now that we've settled that, how about that blowjob…*Jessica?*"

She laughed, even while she undid his zipper. "I'm sorry to inform you that Jessica is gone. You've got Holly Lawson now, and she's not going anywhere."

"I have no complaints with that." He moaned as she slid her hand underneath the waistband of his boxers. "No complaints at all, sweetheart."

The End

Up next: Will's story! Keep reading for *Heat of the Storm…*

Heat of the Storm

An Out of Uniform Novella

Elle Kennedy

Chapter One

WICKED HANDS.

Wet tongue.

Body aching, pulsing, throbbing.

The erotic images jolted Mackenzie Ward out of an already agitated sleep. Outside her rambling old ranch house, the wind howled, slapped against the shingles of the ancient roof and shook the walls with a ferocity that had her heart pounding faster. Rain slid over the windowpanes, leaving wet streaks on the glass, and the ominous rumbling of thunder and white flashes of lightning were a startling combination of light and dark, silence and chaos.

She hated storms. When she was a kid, the arrival of a thunderstorm would send her running into her older sister's bedroom, where she'd burrow under the covers with Alice, shut her eyes and wait for the powerful display of nature to subside.

Nowadays she didn't cower. Tonight's storm was violent, but it wasn't what woke her. Oh no. The carnal vision was responsible for that.

It wasn't a vision.

She said the words in her head a few times, hoping the repetition would convince her brain the images that had just flashed through it were not of the psychic variety. But both mind and body refused to accept it.

The physical symptoms were there—dizziness, numbness in her fingers and toes, the burning in her temples that was neither painful nor pleasant. Her brain also showed signs of extrasensory activity. She could practically feel it humming.

It wasn't a vision.

With a sigh, she hopped out of bed and headed for the door. The hardwood floor under her bare feet was icy, prompting her to slip into a pair of thick wool socks before descending the stairs and heading for the kitchen.

She brewed herself a cup of herbal tea and leaned against the large cedar work island in the middle of the country-style room.

Warm lips dragging over fevered flesh...

"No," she whispered.

It was too late. Her body reacted instantly. Nipples hardened into tight peaks, thighs trembled, stomach clenched. Damn it. It wasn't like she was hard up for sex or anything. She'd only broken up with Dan a couple of weeks ago. Her body shouldn't be this hungry.

Just a dream, she told herself. Because no way would she have had a vision about Will Charleston. *Will*, for God's sake. Her best friend. The one man in her life she'd always been able to count on. He was the broad shoulder she leaned on, the ear she whispered her secrets into, the arms that caught her when she fell. He wasn't the man she'd envisioned having wild animal sex with. He couldn't be.

Even after years of living with this gift—and she used the term loosely—she still wasn't entirely sure how it worked. The images came and went. Sometimes a mundane detail, like the image of Amy, the owner of the bakery, burning a rack of brownies. Other times the images were more troubling. A car accident, her neighbor Mrs. Harrison breaking her back, a death. Visions of the future and always the future of others—she'd never seen herself in a vision.

Which meant that this had all been a dream. A figment of her imagination. She'd only imagined her naked body sprawled across cool white sheets, devoured by Will's talented mouth and eager hands. Only imagined the delicious stretching of her body as his thick cock penetrated her.

A dream.

A wicked dream that wasn't going to come true. Especially not tonight.

She sipped her tea, the hot liquid warming her insides. The storm continued to rage, the wind shrieked, and the rain pounded and pounded and—

The pounding grew louder. It took a moment to realize that it wasn't the rain after all. Someone was knocking on the door.

A vine of wariness climbed up her throat. She'd taken two steps toward the kitchen doorway when her eyesight blurred. Temples throbbed.

Long fingers gripping her ass, digging into her flesh.

Hot mouth clasping over a rigid nipple.

I want you, Mackenzie. Now. Always.

She swallowed hard. What was happening? She couldn't shut out the mental assault, the seductive images prickling her mind like dozens of little bee stings.

The knocking grew incessant.

Sucking in a breath, she walked to the front door and reached for the knob. Her fingers froze over the metal as a rush of heat suddenly torpedoed into her and settled between her legs.

"Who's there?" she called shakily.

"Mac, open up. I'm getting drenched out here."

No. Oh God, no.

"Let me in, Mackenzie."

She slowly opened the door, then stepped aside as a very wet Will Charleston pushed his way inside.

"What are you doing here?" she blurted out. "It's past midnight. And in case you hadn't noticed, there's a hurricane out there."

"Thunderstorm," he corrected. "It was a bitch driving all the way out here from Coronado in this rain, but I needed to see you."

Her mouth grew dry. "Why? What's so important that you risked getting into a car accident over?"

"I think you know."

Four words. Smoky with seduction and shrouded with sinful promise.

This couldn't be happening.

And yet everything about the situation, everything about *him*, spoke otherwise.

His dark eyes glimmered with passion. His sensual mouth was set in a firm line, his defined jaw tight, as if he'd come here prepared for her to fight him. She'd never seen Will like this before. Raw masculinity oozed out of his pores. It teased her, taunted at her, caused every nerve in her body to tingle.

He shrugged out of his navy-blue windbreaker and tossed it on the wooden bench next to the door. Next he kicked off his boots. Drops of rain slid from his dark hair, down his rugged face and dripped onto the floor.

He strode into the living room without invitation. Not that he needed one. Will had always been welcome in her home and he was there often, filling the house with his comforting presence.

Tonight she wasn't comforted. Tonight his presence was…different. Masculine. Dangerous.

"It's time we talked about what happened last week," he said in that rough voice of his.

She gulped. "Nothing happened last week." Fuck, why did he have to bring it up? She'd hoped that during the past seven days, while he'd been traipsing around in the jungle, he might have forgotten about it.

He tilted his head, those bottomless dark eyes piercing right through the lie and glittering with challenge. "I beg to differ."

He moved closer and the spicy scent of his aftershave wafted into her nostrils. She inhaled it, nearly keeling over backwards as the sexy aroma surrounded her and grasped her senses. God, he smelled good.

"You kissed me," he said gruffly.

"It was a mistake."

"We both know that's not true." Another step toward her. "Do you know that this past week has been torture for me? You *kissed* me, Mac, and the next morning I had to get on a chopper, without getting the chance to talk to you about it." He visibly swallowed. "The entire time I was gone, I was thinking about you. Aching for you. So don't try to shrug it off or call it a mistake. Because we both know it wasn't."

Warm hands cupping her breasts.

A pinch to her nipples.

Pain.

Pleasure.

Her thighs squeezed together and a gasp escaped her lips.

He was at her side in an instant, stroking her temples with his long fingers. "Hey, you all right?"

"I'm fine," she squeezed out.

"What did you see?"

Damn it, why did he have to know her so well? She wished she'd never confided in him about the visions. Past experience told her that most people didn't understand them. Hell, she didn't understand them, either.

What she did understand was that it scared people. Men, especially. Her previous boyfriends couldn't handle the visions. They fled the moment a particularly upsetting one hit her, like she was the angel of death or something. Though they vehemently denied it, claiming they were dumping her for an entirely different reason, she knew they considered her a freak.

And hell, sometimes she didn't blame them. Sometimes, usually after seeing something she really didn't want to see, she *felt* like a freak.

"What did you see?" Will repeated.

Their gazes collided and the fire she saw in his eyes stole her breath. He was so sexy. Magnetic eyes, chiseled features, and a sexy body that looked way too good in a pair of faded jeans and a snug T-shirt. His job as a SEAL assured that he always stayed in shape—hard, sleek, and muscled.

Will was the best-looking man she'd ever known, and the one man she'd never allowed herself to get involved with. Her lovers never stayed in her life long. Her best friend? He was always by her side.

But would he remain there if he knew her intimately? If they shared a bed, if she woke him up from sleep with her gasps and tears after a nasty vision? Not to mention her complete inability to lose control in the bedroom. Mackenzie wasn't one to give in to self-pity, but when it came to relationships, she was a mess. A total mess.

And it would crush her, losing her best friend just because she'd been stupid enough to fuck him.

"Either we talk about what you saw, or we talk about the kiss." Will's brows were drawn together in a frown. "Your choice, Mac."

Neither. She wanted to talk about neither.

She edged toward the oversized leather sofa, hoping he'd take her silence and attempt at creating distance between them as a sign to back off. But the words *back off* were not part of his vocabulary and he only stepped closer, so that she was trapped between his big, hard body and the arm of the couch.

"Why did you kiss me?" he asked roughly.

She found the courage to meet his gaze. "I was upset about the break-up with Dan. And drunk. Very, very drunk. I…wasn't thinking."

He didn't answer for a long while. So long that she didn't think he would even reply. She was right. He *didn't* reply. Instead, he grasped her chin with his hands and covered her mouth with his.

The kiss was scarier than the vision. The kiss was *real*.

She was helpless to fight it, though the ache between her legs wouldn't have let her fight anyway. Will's hot mouth rubbed over hers in a slow kiss, his lips firm but deliciously soft, his fingers warm against her cheeks. He deepened the kiss, thrusting his tongue between her lips. He sought out her tongue and swirled over it, the taste of him making her knees wobble.

He immediately slid one hand to her waist to hold her steady. His fingers curled over her hip, his touch searing through the cotton material of her nightshirt and scorching her skin.

She couldn't move. Couldn't think. All she was capable of doing was sagging into his hard chest and drowning in his intoxicating lips.

The kiss grew harder, greedy, almost frantic. He licked her bottom lip, then sucked it hard into his mouth, eliciting a whimper from deep in her chest. And his tongue…it was too demanding, too precise as it flicked over hers, thrust in and out of her mouth, mimicking what she knew he wanted to do to her with his cock.

Fire consumed her body, growing hotter and stronger when he shoved one hard thigh between her legs and ground against her throbbing core. The long ridge of his cock pressed into her mound. The thought of having all that hard, male flesh deep inside her made her gasp with pleasure.

"I want you, Mackenzie," he murmured against her trembling lips. "Now. Always."

The words jolted her back to reality.

She stumbled back, nearly tripping over the couch before regaining her equilibrium. She blinked wildly, trying not to look at his flushed face, the wild lust glimmering in his black eyes. This was Will. Her best friend since she was fifteen years old. For God's sake, she couldn't fall into bed with him, no matter how incredible a kisser he was, no matter how much her body shouted for her to do it.

"We can't," she managed, her voice sounding too desperate to her ears.

"We can," he corrected.

Before she could move farther away, he pulled her against him again and cupped her ass, pushing his pelvis against her so she could feel his unmistakable erection. He dipped his head, his lips hovering over her ear, his hot breath fanning over her skin. "You've been doing this to me from the moment I met you, Mac."

"Will—"

"Don't." His breath tickled her earlobe. "Don't make excuses or give me reasons why we can't do this. I've stood patiently on the sidelines for fifteen years, watched you date other men, waited for you to see what's in front of you. I'm tired of waiting."

She swallowed a moan as he took her earlobe into his mouth and sucked on it. Heart thudding against her ribcage, she wondered how it would feel having Will suckle other parts of her body. Her nipples instantly hardened. Her clit swelled.

"You opened the door to this when you kissed me," he said huskily. "And if I didn't think you wanted it, I'd turn around and walk out the door right now. But you want it, Mac. You want it very, very badly."

She lifted her head and looked into his eyes. She'd never seen him like this, so damn sure of himself, so cocky. God help her, but she liked it. And from the look on his face, he knew it. She'd spilled so many secrets to this man. She didn't have many girlfriends, and sharing her deepest darkest fantasies with Will, her closest friend, hadn't seemed wrong at the time. Now it unnerved her, the knowledge that he knew exactly what she wanted from a lover.

He dragged his index finger along the seam of her lips and rotated his hips, his erection rubbing over the thin boxer shorts she'd worn to bed.

"You're turned on, aren't you?"

The word "yes" slipped out before she could stop it.

A faint smile tugged at his mouth. "Maybe we should do something about that."

"You're my best friend," she whispered.

"Not tonight." He gave a decisive nod, punctuated by another thrust of his groin. "Tonight I'm not your friend, Mac. Tonight I'm the man who's going to fuck you senseless."

She moaned.

He merely smiled again, before his eyes narrowed and his features grew taut. "Last chance, Mac. If you want me to leave, say the word. If not, then you can't fight this any longer." He cocked his head, dark eyes cloudy with both anticipation and challenge. "What'll it be?"

She gulped. A part of her wanted to tell him to go, leave before things got out of hand. Another part of her realized that it was too late. This was already out of hand, and the only thing to do now was ride it out.

"Stay," she murmured.

"Very good decision."

He kissed her again, and this time she responded with fervor. As their tongues tangled, she couldn't fight the wave of disbelief flooding through her, the voice that kept reminding her who she was playing tonsil hockey with at the moment. Kissing Will was surreal. Surreal and yet so incredible she didn't think she'd ever get enough.

Outside, the rain continued to pour, slapping at the house. The sound of the pounding rain matched the pounding of her heart, the howl of the wind echoed the desire howling through her body.

She groaned in disappointment when Will broke the kiss, but he ignored the protest and lifted her into his arms. At five-eight, she could hardly be considered petite, but Will made her feel as light as a feather as he carried her up the stairs and across the dark hallway toward her bedroom.

He deposited her on the bed, placed her on the already tangled sheets and shot her a pointed look.

"W-what is it?" she stammered.

"You know what I want, Mac. Give it to me."

Her pulse raced, the *thump-thump* of her heart reverberating in her ears. The taunting rasp of his voice told her exactly what he wanted. What she'd confessed to wanting herself.

She drew a breath and filled her lungs with much-needed oxygen. Then, without breaking the gaze, she shimmied out of her boxers and threw them aside. Her pussy was exposed, smooth and bare from a recent visit to the salon, wet from the arousal Will elicited inside her.

Darkness bathed the bedroom, making it hard to decipher his expression.

"Turn over."

His order coincided with a flash of lightning that illuminated his face and revealed the seductive glimmer in those piercing black eyes.

Without taking off her nightshirt, she rolled over and positioned herself so she was on her hands and knees. She lifted her ass into the air, stifling a moan when she heard him move closer. His clothing rustled, and then his hands caressed her bare bottom.

Shivers scurried down her spine. She waited.

"Will," she murmured.

She flinched when she felt the sting of his palm against her ass.

"No talking." His voice was gravelly. "I want you stay on your knees, stay quiet, while I do what I want with you."

Moisture soaked her inner thighs. Who was this man? It couldn't be Will, couldn't be the man she'd confided in and depended on for so many years. He had become a different person. Demanding, bold, sexy. She ought to be angry at him for talking to her this way, commanding her as if she were nothing more than a warm body solely there for his pleasure, but she wasn't angry. She was turned on. Hot. Aching.

"That's the fantasy, isn't it, baby?" She felt his warm breath on her cheeks, tickling her exposed slit. "You don't want to be in control anymore. You want a man who'll take what he pleases from you."

He was reciting her own words back to her, and each one caused her to grow wetter.

Yes, it was what she wanted. What she'd always wanted. Living with the visions required holding on to every ounce of control and willpower she possessed. She constantly had to keep herself grounded, restrained, if only to preserve her sanity, sanity that was threatened with each new vision. The restraint followed her into the bedroom, caused her to take charge of her sexual encounters so she wouldn't feel vulnerable.

That's how she felt right now. Vulnerable. And with that unfamiliar emotion came a sense of liberation.

"Are you going to be a good girl while I take what I want?" he asked roughly.

She managed a nod.

"Is that a yes?"

"Yes," she choked out.

"Good."

She trembled when his finger slid down the crease of her ass toward her wet slit. He toyed with her opening, dipping his finger into the moisture pooled there. She thrust her butt out, desperate to feel those long, talented fingers inside her, but he ignored the silent request and moved his hand away. His index finger danced north again, this time rubbing her ass, teasing the puckered hole. At the first feel of the erotic invasion, she clamped her teeth down on her bottom lip to stifle a cry of pleasure.

His soft chuckle broke through the silence. "You like it, don't you, baby? My finger inside your tight ass?"

She shuddered. Anticipation so great, so intense, slammed into her and had her sagging against the mattress. "Will," she started, but he silenced her with another gentle slap.

He pushed the tip of his finger into her ass. When a moan escaped her lips, he spanked her again.

Oh God. She wasn't sure she could take any more of this. Her entire body reacted to him. Muscles taut, legs quivering, nipples as hard as icicles.

The hiss of a zipper being tugged down filled the air. Will's finger left her. She heard him slide out of his jeans, the denim making a soft thud as it hit the hardwood floor. She heard the sound of plastic ripping as he rolled on a condom. Lightning flashed against the windowpane. A crash of thunder followed. She held her breath. She waited. And still he made no move to touch her again.

Eagerness coiled in her belly. Her skin was tight, muscles tense, and she knew, any second now, she'd explode. The ripples of her impending orgasm rose to the surface, danced just out of reach.

It seemed like hours before he spoke again.

"You've got such a sweet pussy," he murmured. "I can't wait to fuck it."

She whimpered, wanting to beg him to do it, to slide his cock deep inside her, but she stayed quiet like he'd ordered.

He moved closer, the tip of his dick brushing over her ass cheeks.

Long fingers gripping her ass, digging into her flesh...

She climaxed before he even entered her.

The orgasm sizzled down her spine, bringing with it streaks of lightning and a crash of thunder that had nothing to do with the storm wreaking havoc outside the farmhouse. Dear God. She gasped for air, coming hard and fast, her soft cries and uncontrollable moans filling the bedroom.

She sank forward on her hands, unable to hold herself up, but Will grabbed her hips and forced her to stay in position. He plunged his cock into her, the force of the thrust causing her to gasp again.

"Take it in," he muttered, his fingers clutching her ass. "All of it, Mackenzie."

She inhaled deeply, forcing her muscles to relax. He was big, his cock long and thick as it filled her pussy. With past lovers, she'd only taken in what she wanted, didn't allow them to push the boundaries, but Will didn't give her a choice. He slammed into her roughly.

He gripped her hips tightly and drove into her with a pace that was feverish and wild. Her inner muscles clasped over him. "You're so tight, Mac," he ground out.

Rotating his hips, he slowed the pace, his hand reaching down to find her swollen clit. He rolled the nub between his fingers, massaging it gently.

Arousal spun through her like a tornado, blowing across her flushed skin until she could barely breathe from the heat consuming her body. Will grabbed her hand and brought it up to her clit, forced her to rub the slick flesh. Mackenzie stroked herself, feeling another orgasm swell inside her. His breath was hot on the back of her neck as he pushed his cock into her again, slowly this time. Both arms wrapped around her from behind, and his hands found her breasts. He palmed each one and teased her nipples with his thumbs.

"Yes," she begged. "Like that, touch me just like that." The orgasm fluttered closer, closer, closer...

He pinched her nipples. Hard.

Pain. Pleasure.

She cried out his name as she came again, clawing at the sheets. He thrust into her, out and in and in and out until she had no clue where one orgasm began and another ended. Sweat coated her forehead, her legs felt numb, and her body was on fire.

Will's fingers curled over her hips as he fucked her. She wanted to turn her head and see his expression. Wanted to know if he was as needy and hot and overwhelmed as she was. But when she tried to tilt her head, he tangled his fingers in her hair and forced her to stay put.

A moment later he let out a hoarse cry and shuddered with release. He gave a few more lazy thrusts before finally withdrawing. Her body instantly felt the loss. She whimpered in disappointment and fell onto the mattress, her breasts aching against the material of her nightie.

Rolling onto her back, she looked up at Will, her best friend, the man who'd just rocked her entire world. He still wore his black long-sleeved T-shirt, but sweat coated the front, causing the material to cling to his rippled chest. She lowered her gaze and feasted on his lower body, the firm muscular thighs, the hard cock that had just brought her to a level of pleasure she'd never known.

Swallowing, she locked her gaze with his, floored by the stark desire she saw in his stormy dark eyes.

She managed a hesitant smile, suddenly feeling far too exposed as she lay on the bed in front of him, naked from the waist down. "Well," she started, then cringed at the ridiculous conversation opener. "That was…" she struggled for words, "…nice."

Nice? Yeah right. The word didn't come close to doing justice to what had happened between them.

Will's expression flickered with both approval and amusement. With a crooked grin, he grabbed his collar and peeled the shirt off his spectacular chest.

Moving closer, he swept his tongue over his lower lip and said, "We're just getting started, Mackenzie."

Chapter Two

WILL TOSSED HIS SHIRT ASIDE AND HEADED FOR THE BED. HE'D NEVER seen anything sexier than the sight of Mackenzie lying there, her silky black hair fanned across the pillow underneath her head, her legs spread open wide.

He'd wanted this woman from the second he'd met her in sophomore year. She was fucking gorgeous, with her tousled, raven-colored hair, eyes as blue as a glacier lake, a sexy, leggy body. After she'd promptly relegated him to friend territory, he'd learned to appreciate her other attributes. The sharp wit, the contagious laughter, even the damn visions. Oh, he knew all about the visions, and he was well aware that they were the reason she was determined to fight the attraction between them. She thought her gift scared men away. Maybe it did. But he wasn't *some men*. He was *the* man.

And tonight he intended to show Mackenzie exactly what he had to offer.

Never taking his eyes off her, he lowered his body onto the mattress and pressed it to hers. When he noticed she still wore her thin gray nightshirt, he grabbed the hem and pulled the garment off her. His mouth watered at the sight of her tits. Full, perky, with small rosy nipples that stood to attention the moment his gaze dropped to them.

Mackenzie shivered.

He smiled faintly and reached out to stroke the swell of one breast. "What did you see tonight?" he asked roughly.

She blinked, surprised by the question. "What?"

He massaged one tantalizing breast, enjoying the way her skin flushed under his gentle caress. "The vision in the living room. What did you see?"

"Nothing. There was no vision."

She was lying. He always knew when she was being dishonest, saw it in the way her forehead creased, the way she averted her eyes.

"Tell me what you saw."

"No."

He removed his hand from her breast. Obvious disappointment shone in her eyes. She tried to guide his hand back to her tits, but he set his mouth in a firm line. "Tell me."

A long silence stretched between them. The sound of rain hitting the windowpane filled the dark bedroom, a rhythmic pounding that matched the thudding of his pulse. Mac shifted her head, and her hair tickled the bottom of his chin. He inhaled the scent of lilac and vanilla. The flowery aroma mingled with the sweet scent of sex lingering between them, flooding his senses and making his cock twitch. He wanted to fuck her again, but quickly reined in the urge. Not yet. Not until she told him what she'd seen, what had freaked her out so badly in the living room.

"I saw..." She sucked in a breath, then released it slowly, the warm stream of air heating his collarbone. "I saw you."

He raised one brow. "Me."

"Yes."

"What else?"

"This."

"Be more specific."

She let out a strangled groan. "I saw you fucking me, okay? I felt your cock inside me, your tongue all over my skin, your fingers dragging over every inch of my body. Satisfied?"

"Oh yeah." He touched her chin and forced her to look at him. "Did it scare you?"

"What do you think?"

She sounded so forlorn that he couldn't help but chuckle. "Are you scared now?"

"No."

"Good," he said with a nod. Shifting over, he propped himself up on one elbow and eyed her curiously. "I want to know more."

"I already told you everything. I had a vision of the two of us having sex. What more could you want?"

"I want you to tell me exactly what you saw." He cupped one breast again and squeezed. "And while you tell me, I'm going to make every last detail come true." He saw her hesitation and frowned. "Too late to back out, remember? So start talking, Mac."

Her delicate throat bobbed as she swallowed. "In the vision your mouth was on my breasts."

He moved over so that he was straddling her smooth, firm thighs. His cock nestled against her slick pussy, but he resisted the urge to slide inside that tight paradise. His mouth hovered over her tits as he murmured, "What was I doing?"

"Kissing. Licking."

He dipped his head and trailed open-mouth kisses along her skin. Fuck, he loved the taste of this woman. Sweet, spicy, feminine. His tongue darted out and traced the swell of one breast, then the other. "What else?"

"You were sucking my nipples."

"Hard? Gentle?"

"Hard," she wheezed out. "It…hurt. In a good way. I almost came from the feel of your teeth biting into me."

He ignored the ever-growing hardness between his legs and brought the vision to life. He licked each nipple, flicked his tongue over them, and then drew one deep into his mouth. He sucked, captured the tight bud between his teeth and bit it lightly.

"Like that?"

"Yes," she gasped.

He circled her areola with his tongue, squeezing her other breast with his hand and feeling her heart pounding against his palm. His cock was so stiff he could barely move. He brushed his tongue over her flushed skin, then cupped her breasts and pushed them together so he could feast on both nipples. He was rougher than usual, sucking so hard he thought he might hurt her. But she didn't seem to mind. Instead, she moaned softly, tangled her fingers in his hair, and held onto his head to keep it on her tits.

With a ragged breath, he pulled back. "What else happened in the vision?"

"You kissed your way down my body."

With a satisfied nod, he moved his mouth south. He didn't leave one inch of her smooth, creamy skin unkissed. He circled her belly button with his tongue, rubbed his lips over her hipbones, her flat stomach, all the way down to her bare pussy.

She moaned and arched her hips, thrusting into his waiting mouth.

"Did I lick you in the vision?" he muttered.

She responded with a sigh, which he took as a yes.

Parting her thighs with his palms, he pressed his lips to her and gave her one lazy lick. She tasted so damn sweet he couldn't help but lap up her juices before pushing his tongue inside her wet hole.

"What else?" he demanded, lifting his mouth a fraction of an inch. "What else did I do?"

"You...sucked on my clit."

From the way she choked out the words, he could tell she was having trouble speaking. Good. He wanted her mindless with lust, wanted her to realize the pleasure he could bring her, the pleasure *only* he could bring her.

His pulse drummed in his ears, making it hard to think, breathe, act. But this wasn't about him. This was about Mackenzie. He lowered his lips again and flicked his tongue over her swollen clit. When she bucked her hips, he reached for her legs and lifted each one over his shoulders. He tongued her for a few delicious moments, groaning when she wrapped her legs tighter around his shoulders and locked her ankles together.

Fuck, he didn't know how long he could hold out. His cock was harder than ever, soaked with pre-come and pleading to be inside Mac's tightness again.

With a strangled breath, he raised his head and met her glazed eyes. "Did I make you come in the vision?"

She nodded, her expression tortured and aroused, her cheeks red with desire. "Twice."

He arched a brow. "That's a tall order."

A tiny grin tugged at the corners of her mouth. "I think you can handle it."

"I can handle anything you throw my way, baby."

Will grinned back and dipped his head between her legs before she had a chance to respond.

Latching his lips over her clit, he sucked the tight bud in his mouth.

Mac cried out, the cry transforming into a sexy moan when he shoved one finger deep inside her. He added a second finger, then a third. Fingered her hard while he tongued her sweet spot until a low groan slipped from her throat and she came.

"Oh God... *Will!*"

Satisfaction like he'd never experienced hit him, and his name on her lips made his cock twitch uncontrollably. He nearly blew his load right then and there from the feel of her clit pulsating against his tongue and her inner muscles clamping down on his fingers. She writhed on the bed, saying his name over and over again, and just when he felt her orgasm subside, he moved his other hand to her ass and shoved a finger inside it. Another groan, wild with desire, slipped from her lips and she came a second time.

"Is that what you saw?" he murmured after she'd stopped shuddering.

She replied with a breathy moan.

Smiling, he slid up her body and covered her mouth with his. She kissed him back, her tongue eager and greedy as it explored every crevice of his mouth. He could still taste her on his lips, and knowing she could taste it too quickened his pulse and drove him fucking wild.

"I saw a lot more," she whispered against his lips.

"Yeah? Tell me."

"No. I'd rather show you."

With the hint of a smile, she slid her hand between their slick, naked bodies and curled her fingers over his rock-hard shaft. White-hot pleasure sliced through him at the exact moment a streak of lightning lit up the bedroom. The light washed over Mac's face, and the raw lust he saw flashing across it made his cock jerk in her hand.

She crawled down his body and took his dick into her mouth. His balls tightened at the sight of her rosy lips wrapped around him. His mind swam in a sea of excitement as her warm tongue devoured his cock, licking him from base to tip, grazing the sensitive underside and swirling over his balls. He couldn't count the number of times he'd fantasized about this.

"Do you like what I'm doing?" Her voice came out throaty, making her sound like the seductress she was.

"Oh yeah."

She licked the drop of moisture that squeezed out of his tip and he shuddered. He was dangerously close to coming, so close that he yanked her up by the hair and forced her greedy mouth away from his cock.

Gripping her waist, he ground his cock against her pussy and kissed her roughly. Her arms came up and wrapped around his neck. "I want you inside me again," she said softly.

"No."

Annoyance clouded her face. "Why the hell not?"

"Because we need to get a couple things straight first."

"I already don't like the sound of this."

"Too fucking bad." He locked his gaze with hers. "This isn't going to be one night, Mackenzie."

"Will—"

"You're not going to shove me back in the friend zone when we wake up tomorrow."

From the flicker of guilt in her eyes, he realized that's exactly what she'd planned to do. Chalk this up to a one-night-stand, or maybe a fluke, and try to make things go back to normal. He knew her too damn well, knew how her mind worked, and right now, her mind continued to hold on to the fear that he'd leave her.

The *unfounded* fear. Because he would never leave her. He didn't care about her visions, and he certainly didn't agree with her ridiculous notion that if she let him in, she'd lose him.

Steel lacing his tone, he added, "We belong together."

Her features creased with pain. "You're my best friend."

Frustration coiled inside of him. He was so fucking sick of hearing those words. "So what?" he shot back. "I can be your lover, too." When she tried to edge away, he held on tight. "You won't lose me, damn it. Your visions don't scare me, Mac. I won't walk away from you the next time you see the damn future."

"You don't get it. I can't control what I see, or when I see it." She sounded frazzled.

"I don't expect you to ignore what you see."

"I'm hard to live with."

"You're harder to live without."

"It's hard for me to let go of control in the bedroom."

"You let go tonight."

"Stop being so fucking logical."

He grinned. "I can't help it. We make sense together. You know it's true."

She looked like she was about to argue, so he silenced her with a kiss. While his tongue tangled with hers, he stroked her breasts with one hand, while moving the other between her legs. She moaned the second his fingers brushed over her clit, and he decided maybe it was time to show her again. Show her how well they fit together, how fiercely he could turn her on, how much she needed him by her side.

He grabbed another condom and quickly put it on, then flipped her over onto her back and crushed her body with his. Without giving her time to react, he slid his entire length inside her. She gasped, then lifted her pelvis to draw him in deeper.

Shaking his head, he grasped her hips to stop her from moving. "Tell me you want to be with me."

The command elicited an annoyed groan from her. She tried bucking up again, but he held her in place.

"Tell me."

"Will—"

"Say it. Say you want to be with me."

"I…" He watched her face, saw the myriad of emotions flickering in her eyes. "I…"

Fear. Her expression shone with fear. Damn it. She still thought she would lose him if she gave in. After everything that had just happened, she still believed he would be like all the other assholes in her life and leave her.

"Say it," he pleaded.

She swallowed, then stared up at him with regret. "I can't," she whispered.

Before he could reply, she wiggled out from underneath him, leaving his cock and his heart aching for her.

"I *can't*," she repeated, and then hurried out of the bedroom.

A second later, he heard the bathroom door in the hallway slam shut.

MACKENZIE SANK DOWN ON THE CLOSED TOILET SEAT, BURYING HER face in her hands and trying unbelievably hard not to cry. The voices in her head screamed at her to go back to the bedroom, but she couldn't do it. Couldn't face Will, couldn't stand to see the love and frustration in his eyes.

Tonight had been a mistake. She shouldn't have given in to her desire. She should've tried harder to resist him.

Say you want to be with me.

The sound of his smoky voice filled her mind, bringing tears to her eyes. Outside, the storm continued to wail, making it difficult to hear anything but the rain against the window and the wind rocking the house. But she could imagine what was going on in the bedroom. Will gathering his clothes, zipping up his jeans. His Windbreaker rustling as he slid it over his powerful shoulders.

She'd hurt him by refusing to say what he wanted. But although the idea of causing Will pain made the tears fall faster, she couldn't give him what he wanted.

He didn't understand. He claimed to, but how could he? So far, he'd only seen what she'd allowed him to see. He'd never been with her when a vision of death came, and no matter how many times he insisted it wouldn't bother him, she knew it would.

Dan had said the same thing, and look what happened with him.

The memory of that night two weeks ago flooded her brain. Someone from town, an elderly man named Colin Garber, had died that night. Burned to death in his bed after his house had caught fire.

And across town, Mac had been in bed with Dan, asleep after a slightly bland lovemaking session. Only to be woken up by images of fire and pain. She could *smell* the smoke, *feel* the heat of the flames as they'd devoured poor Mr. Garber. She hadn't been able to make it to the bathroom, and, mortified, she'd thrown up at the side of the bed. It was a common physical reaction to a violent vision, the nausea, the shortness of breath, the uncontrollable sobs.

It had been too much for Dan. He'd broken things off that night.

No matter how hard she tried, she couldn't believe it would be any different with Will. Oh, he might pretend it didn't freak him out, stick it out for a week, a month, maybe even a year. But eventually he'd get sick of it. Of her, and the visions, and the constant chaos.

Better to put a stop to this now, before…before what? Before she lost her best friend?

She laughed humorlessly. After tonight, she'd probably lost him anyway.

The sound of footsteps in the hall confirmed that devastating thought. Lifting her head, she listened, waited for him to approach the bathroom door, but he didn't. A creak sounded, indicating he'd passed the noisy fourth step on the staircase. Then a few seconds of silence, finally followed by the front door shutting.

Tears poured down Mackenzie's cheeks. He'd left. Not that she was surprised. She'd all but thrown him out.

But it still hurt.

Legs shaking, she rose and approached the sink. She stared at her reflection in the mirror, taking in the sight of her red-rimmed eyes, wet cheeks and tousled hair.

"Congrats," she mumbled to herself. "You officially drove away the one man who's always—"

Pain exploded in her temples.

Then the vision came.

Chapter Three

"OH MY GOD, WILL, HAVE YOU EVER SEEN A MORE GLORIOUS KITCHEN?"
Will glanced around the room in bafflement. A long cedar work island, stainless steel appliances, a table, some cupboards, a small pantry. Looked like an ordinary kitchen to him. Then again, he wasn't a chef, and the only time he used his own kitchen was to shove Chinese takeout boxes in the fridge. He didn't even do dishes, just bought paper plates and tossed them in the trash when he finished eating.

"It's nice," he said, trying to sound impressed.

Holly Lawson's eyes widened in disbelief. "Nice? Are you kidding me? This kitchen is twice the size of the one in my old apartment." She shivered. "Jeez, I'm close to orgasm just looking at it."

The last thing he wanted to hear was the word "orgasm" coming out of his friend's girlfriend's mouth. Not that he didn't like Holly. She was a great girl, but talking sex with her seemed weird.

He watched as she dashed toward the stove and started running her fingers over the burners. She turned around, her brown hair falling into her wide-set green eyes. "Is this not the best stove ever?"

"Yes?"

"*Yes.* I swear, Will, don't you possess a single domestic bone in that big, strong body of yours?"

A blond head poked into the kitchen. "Are you flirting with my lieutenant?" Carson Scott demanded, glaring at his girlfriend.

Holly shot him an innocent smile. "Of course not."

"So you didn't just comment on his big, strong bod?"

"I was just stating the obvious, Carson. He's got a nice body."

Carson studied Will for a moment. "Yeah, I guess you're right."

"Hello, I'm in the room," he said, waving his hand around. "Will the two of you please stop staring at my big, strong body?" He moved toward the door. "Or better yet, give me something to do, because I'm sick of standing around here doing nothing."

He wasn't sure why he'd even agreed to help the couple move. He usually spent all his free time up in Hunter Ridge visiting with Mackenzie, but after what happened last weekend…

He quickly pushed away the memory, knowing if he let the dirty images surface, he'd soon be standing in the middle of Carson and Holly's big, glorious kitchen with a big, glorious hard-on.

Best to focus on the anger, and not the arousal, the night had left him with. He'd been so close, so fucking close to finally getting the woman he'd dreamed about for fucking ages.

Why was she fighting it? Even after they'd experienced the best sex of both their lives, she still wouldn't let him love her.

Hadn't he proved that he would stick by her side? That he didn't care about her visions or think she was a freak?

But Mac had convinced herself she would lose him if she crossed the line from friendship to romance. A part of him didn't blame her, given her past relationships. But all those men she'd dated, well, they were cowards. What kind of man walked away from a woman he cared about because she had a few gruesome visions? As a SEAL, Will had seen his share of gruesome. Hell, the images he encountered on the job were probably far nastier than the ones Mackenzie saw in her head. And still she foolishly believed he was like all the others, that her visions were too tough a pill for him to swallow. She'd deluded herself into it so deeply that she'd had the nerve to ask him to leave—after he'd proven he could turn her on like nobody's fucking business.

And he had no clue how to change her mind. Hot sex hadn't done it, so really, what fucking more could he do?

"You can help Garrett bring in the boxes from the truck," Carson said, interrupting Will's thoughts.

"No," Holly protested. "I need Will to help me and Shelby unpack the kitchen boxes. You help Garrett."

Will was wary as Carson nodded and hurried off, leaving him alone with Holly. The barely restrained smile on her face told him she was up to something, and when Shelby Garrett walked into the kitchen a second later with a smile of her own, Will knew exactly what was going on. These infuriating females had cooked up another matchmaking scheme.

"Sit," Holly ordered, pointing to one of the tall stools by the island. He crossed his arms over his chest. "No."

Shelby marched up to him, curled her fingers over his arm and dragged him to the stool. Her blue eyes twinkled as she forced him to sit. "Come on, just hear us out."

Hear them out? No, thank you. For the past six months, the two women had tried setting him up with a half dozen of their friends, and no matter how hard he fought their constant interference, they couldn't accept that he wasn't interested in being set up.

He supposed this was all his fault. Up until six months ago, he'd avoided forming deeper friendships with the guys on his SEAL team. Not because he was antisocial or anything. He just tended to keep to himself, and he enjoyed driving up to Hunter Ridge in his free time and hanging out with Mackenzie rather than staying near the base with the other guys.

But after Garrett married Shelby, things had changed. Suddenly Will was forced to attend a bachelor party and a wedding. And then Carson, for some reason, decided to start inviting him to play golf and go out for drinks. Before he knew it, he was eating dinner at Shelby and Garrett's every Wednesday night, and helping Holly and Carson move into their new Coronado bungalow.

Whether he liked it or not, they were his friends. Though he didn't quite understand why Shelby and Holly had decided to focus all their matchmaking attentions on him. Ryan and Matt, two other guys from his SEAL team, were also single, but he didn't see *them* getting harassed.

"Okay," Shelby began, flipping her blonde ponytail over her shoulder. "There's a new waitress at the restaurant where Holly works, and we think this girl is perfect for you."

Will rested his elbows on the cedar counter and sighed. "Really?"

"Really," Holly chimed in. "Her name is Lisa, she's gorgeous, and she's studying to become a massage therapist."

"A massage therapist!" Shelby echoed. "Think of all the things she could do to your body!"

Will had to laugh.

"Oh, and she's a really good cook," Holly added. "Also, she speaks three languages."

Shelby wiggled her eyebrows. "Dirty talk in *three* languages, Will. How can you pass this up?"

Well, their pitch was pretty good, what with the massages and foreign dirty talk, but unfortunately, Will had no desire to go out with this woman. His heart would always belong to Mac.

"It sounds...tempting," he lied. "But I'm going to pass."

He was met by two identical crestfallen expressions.

"Why?" Holly burst out.

"You know why," he said with a shrug.

Shelby let out a frustrated sigh. "Ugh! Aren't you over that woman yet?"

"Nope. If anything, I'm more in love with her than ever. We slept together last weekend."

He hadn't planned on revealing what happened between him and Mac, especially not to these two nosy women, but somehow the entire story spilled out. Fists clenched to his sides, he told them about his night with Mackenzie and the disappointing way it had ended.

"What is the *matter* with her?" Holly grumbled when he was done.

"She takes him for granted, that's what," Shelby answered angrily. "Seriously, Will, how are you still putting up with this? She doesn't deserve you."

"Yeah, she does."

Shelby leaned against the counter, frowning. "You honestly think Mackenzie is worth all this heartache?"

"Yeah, she is."

A short silence fell over the kitchen, finally broken by the sound of Shelby slapping her hand on the counter. "Then it's time we do something about it."

Will narrowed his eyes. "We?"

"Yes, we." She shot him a grin. "Obviously you're not having too much success on your own, so it's time someone stepped in and helped you."

He held up a warning hand. "No fucking way. You guys are *not* stepping in. Mac and I will straighten this out by ourselves."

Holly snorted, the determined glint in her green eyes telling him exactly whose side she was on. Not his. "Shelby's right, you need our help."

Sliding off the chair, he edged his way to the doorway. "The two of you are not getting involved in my love life."

Another snort from Holly, and a giggle from Shelby. "What love life?" they said in unison.

He stabbed a finger in their direction. "The answer is no. I don't need or want your help. I'm serious about this."

Shelby and Holly exchanged a look.

"I'm serious," he insisted. "I command you to put a pin in whatever scheme you two are about to cook up. Stay out of my business—that's an order."

With that, he strode out of the kitchen, for all the good it did him. He could hear Shelby and Holly already whispering to one another, and if he knew those two, they'd show up at his door tomorrow morning with some hare-brained plot that would no doubt make his life miserable.

Though how his life could get more miserable than it already was, he didn't know.

WILL WAS GOING TO DIE.

Mackenzie wandered around her kitchen on autopilot, brewing a cup of tea, eating but not really tasting a piece of toast. Staring at the sunlight streaming in from the window. Doing the dishes.

All the while, her mind was somewhere else. Somewhere dark and terrifying. A place that held not even the tiniest flicker of hope. A world without Will.

With a strangled groan, she sank into one of the chairs around the kitchen table and buried her face in her hands, a position she'd found herself in often over the past five days. She hadn't heard from Will since he'd walked out that night, and a part of her almost wished his silence dragged on a bit longer.

What was she supposed to say if he called?

Did she tell him what she'd seen?

But how could she? She'd tried warning people before when she had a vision about them, but no matter what she did, the visions always came true. She couldn't change them. Couldn't stop them.

And what she'd seen... She wished like hell she could stop it.

The gunshots. The shriek of the helicopter rotors, the heart-stopping explosion rocking the chopper.

The smoke.

Helicopter falling from the sky, hurtling toward the canopy of green below.

A sob choked her throat as Will's face flashed across her mind. The grim realization in his dark eyes when he realized his fate. When he accepted it.

"No!" she burst out, shooting to her feet.

It wouldn't happen. It *couldn't* happen.

Say you want to be with me.

Why, *why* hadn't she been able to say it? She'd already crossed a line anyway and slept with her best friend, so why couldn't she take that final step and admit what they both knew to be true?

Because you don't want to lose him.

No, she definitely didn't want that. Will was the only steady male in her life. Even after he'd joined the Navy and left town, he always came back. Weekends, holidays, any time he could get leave, he came back to Hunter Ridge. To her.

Would he come back this time? After everything that happened last week?

And what would she say to him if he did?

Hey, Will, I acted like an idiot. The sex was incredible, the best of my life. And oh, you're going to die.

She paced the kitchen, her bare feet slapping against the hardwood floor, as her heart pounded against her ribs in a steady rhythm of panic. She had to tell him. Warn him. So what if he was probably furious with her? Maybe if she said something, she could change what she'd seen.

Lifting her chin in determination, she grabbed her phone from the counter. She jumped when it started ringing in her hand.

Hope bloomed in her chest. Quickly pressing the *talk* button, she lifted the phone to her ear and said, "Thank God you called!"

There was a beat, then a soft female chuckle. "Why do I get the feeling you were expecting someone else?" came Paula Durtz's amused voice.

Disappointment jolted through her. "Oh. Hi, Paula. I, um…what's up?"

"I just wanted to see if you're still coming into town today."

Town? Oh, right, she'd promised to drop off that necklace for Paula. "What time did we say again?" Mac asked.

"Two. So are we still on?"

She glanced at the clock hanging over the sink. It was quarter to, which meant she needed to get going. Yet the idea of leaving the house troubled her. She wasn't in the mood for socializing, not when she couldn't stop thinking about Will. About what it would cost her if she lost him. Actually *lost* him.

But Paula was the closest thing to a friend she had in Hunter Ridge. Maybe if she talked to her, told Paula what she'd seen…? Maybe the older woman could offer some advice.

"Yeah, we're on," Mac said. "I'll meet you in the square in fifteen."

Chapter Four

"I LOVE IT," PAULA DECLARED FIFTEEN MINUTES LATER, HOLDING UP THE pendant to admire it. The late afternoon sun caught on the little gold heart, making it sparkle.

Mackenzie gave a wry smile. "You hate it, and we both know it. It's not your style at all."

She emphasized the last remark with a pointed look at all the jewelry currently draped over various parts of the other woman's body. A chunky silver necklace hung around Paula's neck, and the numerous bracelets around her wrists boasted colorful costume gems and dangling charms. Even Paula's wedding ring, a thin silver band encrusted with little diamonds, was elaborate in comparison to the simple necklace Mac had created for her. Not that Paula's accessories were gaudy—if anything, Mac's necklace was just too plain.

Paula laughed. "If it's not my style, then why did you make it for me?"

"Because it's as far as my skill can take me," she grumbled.

"Well, if you'd just let me pay you for reading my fortune, then we wouldn't have to go through this jewelry pretense, now would we, hon?" The lines around Paula's mouth creased in amusement. "Don't get me wrong—I'm willing to buy all the necklaces you want to make me. But don't kid yourself, Mackenzie Ward. You're not a jewelry maker, plain and simple. You're a psychic."

Mac tried not to flinch. She hated that word. *Hated* it. She wasn't in denial; she was quite aware that her visions did indeed make her psychic. She simply didn't like thinking of herself as that. Ever since she was a little girl, she'd struggled with her *gift*. She despised the visions. Didn't need 'em, didn't want 'em. As an adult, she'd tried hard to distance herself from them.

She'd graduated from high school, gone to college, learned how to make jewelry. She'd moved back to Hunter Ridge determined to work on her craft and start a business, and though the townsfolk humored her by buying her pieces, Mackenzie wasn't stupid. She knew they only cared about her psychic abilities. She also knew most of them thought she was a nut job. They might chat with her in the supermarket or strike up friendly conversations at the local bar, but their minds were always on her "gift". Wondering if she'd seen something terrible happen to them, thinking of a way to ask her about their future without looking like that's all they wanted.

Only a few people seemed to genuinely care about her, visions or not. Paula was one of them. Will was another.

An ache seized her chest at the thought of Will.

Helicopter falling from the sky...

"Mackenzie? Honey, you okay?"

Paula's voice sliced through her painful thoughts. She turned away from the woman's concerned gaze, pretending to focus on a few fat pigeons sitting on the large fountain in the middle of the town square.

It was a gorgeous day, the sun high in the blue, cloudless sky, a warm breeze floating through the town. You'd never think a fierce storm had passed through here less than a week ago, but it had, and along with turning Mac's entire world upside down, she'd heard the town had suffered some damage too. Lightning had struck one of the shops on idyllic Main Street, and a tree had cracked in two and smashed into the roof of the bowling alley.

When Mac had gone into town the next day, a few people even had the audacity to ask her why she hadn't seen the storm coming. Fuckers. Like her visions could be controlled.

"Don't be angry with me, hon."

She nearly fell off the bench when she felt Paula's hand on her knee. With a strained smile, she said, "I'm not angry with you. I was just thinking about the storm last weekend."

Paula smiled knowingly. "Will was in town then, wasn't he?"

Mackenzie wasn't surprised that the other woman knew about Will's visit. Paula owned the one and only general store in town, which ensured she knew everything that went on in Hunter Ridge. Ever since her husband died two years ago, Paula had thrown herself into that store, and she rarely closed shop before two in the morning. Since Will would've had to drive through Main Street when he got in, Paula would've noticed his car. She noticed everything.

"Yeah, he was here," Mac admitted.

"Did you two have a nice visit?"

"Not really." She shrugged. "We fought."

Paula raised her eyebrows. "I don't believe that. You and Will have been inseparable since high school. I don't think I've ever seen you so much as raise your voices at one another."

"There's a first time for everything, I guess."

Oh, yeah, definitely a first time for everything—like having mind-blowing sex with her best friend.

"But you made up, right?"

"Actually, I haven't seen or spoken to him since," Mac said evenly.

She wished the bitterness in her voice wasn't so obvious, but she couldn't help it. Yes, Will's stony departure had been her fault. She'd refused to open her heart to him, to give him what he wanted, and she didn't blame him for being mad. But not even a phone call since he'd left? She knew he wasn't out of the country, since he always called or texted her before he went away, so the silence on his part bothered her.

"This is silly. Call him up, Mackenzie," Paula ordered, her curly brown hair bouncing on her forehead as she shook her head. "You and Will love each other."

That's the problem.

She didn't voice the thought, just offered a tense smile and said, "Can I ask you something?"

"Of course. Anything."

She hesitated. "If I saw…if I told you I'd seen something dark in your future, would you want to know?"

Paula's face went pale. "Oh dear Lord! You saw my death!"

Mac quickly patted the woman's arm. "No, not at all. I promise. This is strictly hypothetical."

Paula visibly relaxed. "Wait. You're thinking about poor Mr. Garber, aren't you?"

"Yeah," Mac lied.

"Aw, honey. You know you shouldn't feel guilty about what happened. You couldn't stop it."

"No, I couldn't," she said sadly. "The vision came too fast. He died before I could even call the police." She swallowed. "But if I saw something ahead of time, about you—hypothetically—would you want to be warned? Even if you knew it was set in stone?"

Paula paused thoughtfully. "Is it really, though? Set in stone, I mean?"

Tears stung Mac's eyes. "So far. I've never seen anything that didn't happen. It always comes true, Paula. Always."

"Then, yes." Paula gave a brisk nod. "I would want to know."

"Really?"

"Sure. I'd get my affairs in order. Make amends. Leave nothing unsaid. I'd want to enjoy every second I had left."

Mac fell silent, wondering if that's what Will would do. Straighten his affairs, enjoy his last moments?

Somehow she couldn't picture it. Knowing Will, he'd push everyone away—for their own good, of course. He'd say a quick goodbye and disappear, wanting to protect the people in his life from unnecessary heartache.

And although she hadn't seen or spoken to him in days, the thought of him leaving turned her insides. If he knew he was going to die, he would push her away, while she would want nothing more than to keep him as close as she could.

A helicopter falling from the sky…

She shoved the horrific image aside and straightened her shoulders. She might not be able to change the future, but she sure as hell could change the present.

"Tomorrow," she announced.

The older woman looked startled. "What?"

"If I don't hear from Will tonight, I'm calling him first thing tomorrow."

Paula grinned. "Good girl."

Mac drew in a calming breath and repeated the word in her head. *Tomorrow.*

"So?"

Will stared into Shelby's excited blue eyes and wondered if he was nuts for actually seeing the merit of this crazy scheme. It didn't help that he was feeling pretty disoriented, considering the two women had come knocking on his door at six in the morning and interrupted his much-needed sleep. He hadn't slept much since his night with Mackenzie. Too much tossing and turning and cursing her for being so damn stubborn.

With a groan, he rubbed his tired eyes and rose from the couch, where Holly and Shelby had sandwiched him after he'd led them into the tiny living room of his even tinier bungalow. This place had never quite felt like home to him. It kept him close to the base, but that was the only draw about it. To him, home was Hunter Ridge. And not the two-story redbrick house he'd grown up in, which was now occupied by another family. Nope. Home was Mackenzie's creaky old farmhouse, the only place where he felt truly like himself.

Home was Mackenzie.

"Come on, Will," Holly said as she trailed after him into the kitchen. "You know this is a good plan."

"You know it is," Shelby chimed in.

"Would you at least let me make a cup of coffee before we discuss this juvenile bullshit?" he grumbled. Striding over to the counter, he clicked on the coffeemaker and then grabbed a mug from the cabinet over the sink. "You guys want any?"

Both women shook their heads, then waited patiently as he fixed himself a cup of black coffee. But he could see the unrestrained enthusiasm in their eyes. Leaning against the fridge, he gulped down the scalding liquid and waited for the java to do its thing. Almost instantly he felt alert, his mind sharpened by the caffeine. But while the sharp mind should've kick-started his usually excellent common sense, he still found himself intrigued by the women's ridiculous plan.

Obviously picking up on his interest, Shelby gave a delighted laugh. "You think it'll work, don't you?"

Sipping his coffee, he eyed them over the rim of his mug. "I'll admit, it's not a bad idea."

Holly grinned. "So when do we leave?"

He scratched the stubble on his chin with his free hand. "I'm not saying I'll do it."

"Of course you'll do it," Holly said. Her grin widened. "This is going to be so much fun."

Will eyed the brunette. "Have you spoken to Carson about this idea? You know, your *live-in boyfriend*? I hardly think he's going to agree to this."

Holly shrugged. "Sure he will. He's been saying for ages how you need to settle down."

"I'm perfectly willing to settle down. It's the woman I want to settle down with who's not being cooperative."

"Which is why we're going to kick some sense into her stubborn head," Holly said breezily. "Trust me, no woman wants to see the man she loves with another woman. The claws always come out when a chick feels threatened."

Will chuckled. "Sure you want to face those claws, Hol? Mac's a lot tougher than you think."

Holly smirked. "I can handle her."

Next to her, Shelby laughed. "Can I be there when we tell Carson about this?"

"I still haven't agreed," Will interjected, sipping his coffee again.

But the protest was futile, because they all knew he would do it. Childish as this plan was, he suspected it might be exactly what Mackenzie needed. Although he wouldn't go as far as to say she'd taken him for granted, he did believe there was some truth to that.

Since they were fifteen years old, Mac had leaned on him for support. Whether she'd been upset about the visions or complaining about her older sister, who'd been appointed Mac's guardian after their parents died, Will always offered his ear and his shoulder. He'd watched her date other guys, listened to her describe her sexual fantasies, and through it all, Mac had continued to ignore the chemistry between them.

But while she'd had no problem introducing Will to whatever boyfriend she was with at the time, he'd never taken a woman back to Hunter Ridge before. And there had definitely been other women. Warm, willing females with whom he'd passed the time and dated in an attempt to forget Mackenzie.

What would she do if he brought a woman home? Would it tear at her insides the way the sight of her with other men tore at his?

Would she finally find the strength to admit she loved him as much as he loved her?

He didn't know the answer to any of those questions, but he was damn well going to try and get 'em.

He slammed his mug down on the counter and set his jaw. "You know what? Scratch that. I *have* agreed." He fixed a determined stare at Holly. "We leave tomorrow."

"You want to *borrow* my girlfriend?" With an outraged curse, Carson dropped the box in his hands so he could curl both fists and wave them in front of Will.

The cardboard box smashed onto the floor of Carson and Holly's new glorious kitchen with a resounding thunk and the distinct sound of glass shattering.

"My new plates!" Holly wailed, immediately sinking to her knees. She ripped open the tape closing the two flaps together and peered into the box. Then she looked up at Carson in horror. "You're a monster!"

Carson scowled at her. "I'll buy you new plates." The scowl deepened. "That is, if I decide not to break up with you. I can't believe this was your idea. I *told* Garrett you and Shelby shouldn't hang out. The two of you are trouble together."

"They're just trying to help me out," Will pointed out, experiencing a jolt of sympathy at the despair on Holly's face. He swiftly knelt down and tried to pry her hands out of the box. "Quit sticking your fingers in there, Hol. It's filled with broken glass."

Carson released an enraged roar. "Don't you dare comfort my girlfriend. *My* girlfriend!"

Holly got to her feet and planted her hands on her hips. "Now I'm definitely going," she shot back. "You broke my plates."

"So you're going to play house with my lieutenant as punishment?"

"He's in love with another woman!"

"Well, I'm in love with *you*!"

Holly's eyes softened. "Doesn't it make you love me more knowing I'm willing to help one of your friends?"

Carson sighed. "What is it with you and helping people? Didn't we just decide you're not going to drop everything for your family anymore?"

"This isn't my family. It's *yours*."

"Will and I aren't related."

"You're SEALs. Of course you're related."

Another sigh. "Yeah, you're right." Carson took a step forward and pulled Holly into his arms. "Fine, you can go."

"Really?"

"I just said it, didn't I?"

Holly threw her arms around her boyfriend, and the two proceeded to make out as if Will wasn't in the kitchen.

He shook his head to himself. He wasn't really sure how they'd gone from furious to calm to horny in a matter of seconds, but he wasn't complaining. Ever since Holly and Shelby had burst into his house this morning, he'd been warming up to the plan, starting to believe it might actually work. He was glad Carson hadn't put up more of a fight.

Slipping his hands in the pockets of his khakis, he let the couple smooch a while longer, then cleared his throat. "Uh, guys?"

They pulled apart sheepishly. "Sorry," Holly said. "Forgot you were here."

Story of his life, women forgetting he was standing right in front of them.

Hopefully not for much longer, though.

"So how is this going to work?" Carson asked, bending down to retrieve the fallen box. He glanced at his girlfriend. "I'm sorry about the plates, sweetheart. We'll go out and buy some next week, 'kay?"

"I'm holding you to that." With a stern look, she headed for the fridge and grabbed a can of soda. "Anyway, Will and I are going to Hunter Ridge tomorrow. Apparently there's some fair going on this weekend."

"Carnival," Will corrected. "It's an annual thing."

Last year he'd skipped the carnival. Mac had been dating Dan, the owner of the hardware store, and Will wasn't keen on the idea of seeing them. When they were teenagers, he and Mac had always gone to the carnival together. They used to ride the Ferris wheel for hours, talking about everything and anything while they shared a bag of cotton candy. Nothing had changed once they'd gotten older. They still rode that Ferris wheel and munched on that cotton candy every year when the carnival came to town. Last year was the first time he'd missed it.

And this year, well, this year *he'd* be the one with the date. A part of him got perverse satisfaction from knowing Mackenzie would finally feel that same bitter jealousy he'd experienced when she decided to go to the carnival with another man.

"So you're taking my girlfriend to a carnival in your no-horse town?" Carson rolled his eyes. "Sounds like, uh, fun."

"We're going to make Mac jealous," Holly reminded him. "The carnival is their *thing*."

"We'll only be gone for one night," Will said. "I promise to have her back Saturday night."

Carson narrowed his eyes. "And where exactly will the two of you sleep?"

Will shrugged. "Only one place to stay in town. Harriet Jones' B&B."

"Two rooms?"

He glanced at his feet. "One." Before Carson could start yelling again, he quickly added, "I'll sleep on the floor. Fully clothed."

"I'll sleep naked," Holly piped up.

Carson shot her a glare. "If you do, I'll smash every piece of china in this place."

"Fine." She smiled impishly. "I'll wear the black lace teddy you bought me for my birthday."

Will let out a sigh. "That was way too much information." He glanced at Carson. "So are you cool with this, man?"

"Do I have a choice?"

Holly smiled broadly. "No."

Chapter Five

THE CARNIVAL WORKERS WERE SETTING UP WHEN MACKENZIE STRODE out of Paula's general store on Friday afternoon. She wasn't sure how she felt about the carnival this year. It had always been her and Will's thing, except for last year when he'd been out of the country…though a part of her still suspected he'd been happy to miss the event. She'd been dating Dan then, and she'd gotten the feeling Will wasn't comfortable around her ex-boyfriend.

Oh, who was she kidding? Of course he wasn't comfortable. What man would want to spend time with the boyfriend of the woman he loved?

Love. For fifteen years she'd tried not to think about that word, but after what happened between them last week—the staggering, unbelievable sex—she couldn't bury her head in the sand any longer. Will loved her. She'd seen it in his eyes that night, heard it in his voice, felt it in his kiss.

And instead of welcoming that love into her life, she'd slammed a door on it.

Swallowing, she walked toward her car. The sound of the carnival coming to life made her heart ache—the screech of metal as the Ferris wheel cars were tightened into place, the mechanical rings of the game booths, the melody of the carousel as it whirled around on its test runs.

No, she wouldn't be attending this year, she decided as she unlocked the driver's door of the old Chevy. Not when she still hadn't spoken to Will. Not when she didn't know if he would be there.

When she'd called him this morning, she'd gotten beeped over to voice mail. She left a message asking him to call her. He hadn't. She'd called an hour later, left another message. Called a third time. A fourth. And still he hadn't answered.

And each time she'd heard his voice on the message, her panic had escalated. What if he'd left the country? What if she was too late?

By the time afternoon rolled around, she'd been ready to rip her own hair out. So she'd gotten in her car, driven into town to fill up the tank, and was now about to make the drive to Coronado. Screw his voice mail. She needed to see him in person. She had to make sure he was okay

Gripping the steering wheel with icy fingers, Mac inhaled a calming breath and tried to reassure herself that Will was simply avoiding her calls. He hadn't left town. He wasn't sitting on a chopper right now, and he was *not* dead.

The mere word—*dead*—sent panic soaring through her and brought tears to her eyes. No, she refused to think about the vision. Will was fine. Of course he—

A loud honk drew her out of her anxiety. When she turned her head in the direction of the intrusive noise, her anxiousness transformed into pure relief.

An olive-green Jeep pulled into the parking space in front of hers.

Will's Jeep.

Before she could stop herself, she was out of her car and bounding toward the Jeep on shaky legs. Unease, relief and excitement pounded in her veins.

She reached the driver's door just as Will was getting out.

The sight of him caused her belly to do a funny little flip. God, he looked good. So unbelievably good in faded jeans and a close-fitting black T-shirt. But clothes didn't make the man, and she knew from recent personal experience that Will didn't need a stitch of clothing to look good. In fact, he was a female's wet dream when he was naked. Her cheeks burned at the memory.

"You're here," she blurted out.

His dark eyes softened at the sight of her, but then his expression grew shuttered. "Couldn't miss the carnival," he said lightly.

"I...I called you." The twinge of desperation in her voice made her want to cringe. "I left a message."

"Did you?" His tone was cool. "I haven't checked my messages today."

Okay, so he was still angry with her. The stiffness of his impossibly broad shoulders and the distant look in his eyes confirmed it. And he hadn't shaved in days, she noticed. Thick stubble dotted a jaw that was visibly tensed. She wished she knew how to make it better, how to bridge this awful distance between them.

"Will," she murmured. "I'm...sorry."

"Yeah, you said that last week."

"I still feel it."

His dark gaze swept over her face. For a second she glimpsed a glimmer of regret, a flash of desire, but then it snapped back to chilly and distant. "So do I, Mac."

She opened her mouth to respond, but whatever she'd been about to say—she wasn't even sure what—died a fiery death when a flicker of movement caught her eye. Shock barreled into her as she watched someone get out of the passenger side of Will's Jeep.

Not someone.

A *woman*.

And not any woman, but a gorgeous one. A beautiful green-eyed brunette in Capris and a tank top, who marched over to Will's side and possessively linked her arm through his.

"Are you going to introduce me to your friend?" the woman asked with a teasing lilt to her voice.

Mac was frozen in place, unable to take her eyes off their interlocked arms. Will had brought a woman with him? In all the years she'd known him, he'd never shown up in town with someone on his arm. *Never.*

Something fierce and ugly reared up inside her. She suspected that something was jealousy, but there was also a spark of resentment. He was *dating* someone? He'd had sex with her last weekend and now he was dating *someone else*?

"Holly, this is Mackenzie," Will said gruffly. "Mac, Holly."

"It's nice to meet you." The lie flowed smoothly out of Mac's mouth, while the anger flowed just as smoothly through her veins. Damn him for bringing a woman home. How could he do that after everything he'd said and done last week?

I want you, Mackenzie. Now. Always.

Ha!

"So you're the friend Will told me about," Holly replied with a warm smile.

A *genuinely* warm smile. Which meant that Will hadn't told his new girlfriend about the body-numbing sex he'd had with his *friend*.

Mac pressed her hands to the sides of her jeans, resisting the urge to use those hands to wring Will's neck. "Will and I have known each other for years," she answered with forced casualness. "How do the two of you, uh, know each other?"

Holly tightened her grip on Will's arm, her green eyes twinkling as she got up on her tiptoes and brushed her lips over his stubble-covered cheek.

Mac noticed how short the other woman was, and a pang of insecurity tugged at her gut. Compared to Holly's petite, pixie frame, Mac felt like a giant. Suddenly her height of five-eight seemed enormous, all wrong for Will. Will and Holly looked perfect together—tall, muscular Will and little, perfect Holly.

It made her want to throw up.

"We actually just met, um…" Holly tilted her head thoughtfully, "…last Sunday. I work at a restaurant near the base, and Will showed up for lunch. He came back to the kitchen after his meal and complimented my cooking." Holly's cheeks flushed in an annoyingly cute way.

She was a cook. How delightful. Mac couldn't even make an omelet without burning something.

Before her confidence could take another hit, her brain stumbled on what Holly had said—last Sunday. Will had met this girl the day after he'd rocked Mackenzie's world. One day! Was that all he'd needed to put the entire incident out of his mind? Was that why he hadn't called her this week, because he'd been too busy rocking someone else's world? And to think, she'd been frantic about his *safety*. Obviously he was perfectly safe with his new girlfriend.

"Holly just graduated from culinary college," Will said, shrugging his arm from Holly's and slinging it around her shoulder instead.

Mac tried not to stare at the careless way his fingers caressed Holly's bare shoulder. "That's nice," she said. "So…you two are in town for the carnival?"

"Yep," he replied, expressionless.

"Will was telling me all about it," Holly spoke up as she snuggled closer to him. "I had the weekend off, so when he said he wanted to show me where he grew up, I couldn't pass it up." With a naughty smile,

Holly trailed one finger across Will's chest. "I want to know *everything* about you, babe."

Okay, Mac was officially going to be sick.

Taking an awkward step back, she feigned a smile. "Well, you'll have fun. The carnival is always fun." Another step backwards. "I've gotta go. I left my car running." Right, because there was actually a chance one of the straight-laced Hunter Ridge residents might hop into her beat-up Chevy and commit grand theft auto.

"Will you be at the carnival tonight?" Will asked politely.

She continued inching away from the perfect couple. "Um, I'm not sure yet."

"Oh, come!" Holly said with another real-looking smile. "I'd love to get to know Will's best friend."

"Uh…"

"We'll save you a seat on the Ferris wheel," Will told her.

She swallowed down a hysterical laugh. Yeah, like that would inspire her to show up. Sitting on a Ferris wheel with Will and his new *girlfriend* was about as appealing as sticking pins in her eyes.

"Yeah, maybe," she said noncommittally. "If I decide to go, I'll find you guys. Anyway, um…bye."

Tearing her gaze from the two of them, she stumbled back to her car. As she slid into the driver's seat, she was irritated to see that Will and Holly weren't even paying attention to her anymore. Will had planted his hands on Holly's slender hips, and the brunette's arms were now locked around his strong, corded neck. Their bodies were pressed together, their faces inches apart.

Mac averted her eyes before she could witness something she didn't want to see—Will kissing another woman. But the mere thought of it sent waves of jealousy to her gut.

Damn him.

Clenching her teeth so hard her jaw ached, she pulled out of the parking spot and drove away from Main Street as fast as she could.

WILL STARED AT THE REAR BUMPER OF MAC'S CAR AS SHE SPED OFF. Satisfaction settled in his chest, along with a knot of pain that tightened his throat. He'd been so tempted to pull her into his arms when she'd hurried over to his Jeep. She'd looked so relieved, so happy to see him, and as annoyed as he was with her, he'd been happy to see her too. He always felt so empty when he was away from her.

But he'd restrained himself from embracing her, from planting a usual peck on her smooth cheek. He'd brought Holly here for a reason and he wasn't about to blow the charade in its first five minutes. Mac needed to see he wasn't kidding around. He'd waited more than a *decade* for her. Any other man would've given up already, focused his attention on a woman who actually wanted to be with him. But Will had exercised patience, waiting for Mackenzie to get over her fears, hoping she'd finally open her eyes and see that he was the only man for her.

Not even amazing sex had managed to sway her. And the relief he'd glimpsed in her pale blue eyes when she'd walked up to him just now told him she assumed things could go back to normal, that he could put the sex out of his mind and go back to being her best bud. Well, that wasn't going to happen.

Mackenzie would either get all of him or none of him, and hopefully seeing him with another woman would be the kick in the butt she needed. The catalyst that pushed her to take that final step and admit she loved him.

"She is *pissed,*" Holly said with a grin, dropping her hands from his neck.

He stepped back, his gaze still on the now empty road. "Furious," he agreed.

"Should we high-five?"

He laughed. "Not yet. She's still not ready to make a move. I bet right now she's probably trying to convince herself it didn't bother her to see me with you."

Holly shook her head. "If this was me and Carson, and I saw him with someone else, I'd bitch-slap the woman and claim my man."

"She's scared."

"To be loved?"

"To be abandoned." He swallowed. "Every guy she's dated has dumped her when the visions got too scary for him. And this last break-up…it hurt her pretty badly. Dan—the guy she was with—said some seriously shitty things when he broke up with her."

"Like what?"

"She didn't give me all the details, but I got the feeling it was bad. Her vision really freaked him out."

He frowned, wondering if maybe he ought to pay a visit to dear old Dan in the hardware store. Normally he tended to avoid the men Mac dated, but Dan had always rubbed Will the wrong way. And after Colin Garber died in that fire, Dan had definitely made Will's shit list. Instead of comforting Mackenzie, the bastard had thrown her away like a piece of trash.

Then again, the break-up was the reason Mac had kissed him, and the reason he'd driven to her house last weekend. So maybe he should be thanking Dan.

Will shrugged. Nah. He still wanted to unleash a right hook in that creep's jaw.

"Doesn't she know you're a Navy SEAL who doesn't freak out easily?" Holly asked.

"All she knows is that I'm the only man who's always stood by her. She thinks she'll lose me if she opens herself up fully."

"Well, I think she's silly." Holly glanced around the quaint street. "Is there anywhere good to eat around here?"

"There's a bar around the corner. Serves some pretty decent chicken wings. But the diner is where I usually go. All-day breakfast."

"Are you buying?"

"Of course." He chuckled. "Don't tell me Carson makes you guys go Dutch."

"We don't usually go out to eat. The food I cook is better than anything you'll get in a restaurant." She beamed. "Well, my restaurant is the exception, but that's because I'm the chef." She slung her arm through his and pushed him toward the curb. "Come on, let's go. I'm starved."

"YOU ARE NOT GOING TO THE CARNIVAL," MACKENZIE MUTTERED TO

herself, absently wandering around her kitchen looking for something to eat.

Her pantry was stocked with canned food, her freezer loaded with homemade lasagnas that Paula brought over once a month, but nothing looked appealing at the moment. Hard as she tried, she couldn't stop thinking about all the junk food she could have if she went to the carnival. Greasy hamburger, spicy fries from Walter Halton's booth, cotton candy.

She refused to give in to her stomach's demands, though. The last thing she wanted to do was see Will and Holly, arms around each other, secret smiles, kisses…oh God, she didn't even want to imagine them kissing.

Sighing, she opened the fridge and peered inside for the third time, but like the two previous glimpses, it remained empty save for a carton of milk and a few condiments. She was just closing the fridge door when her hands started to tingle. Her temples ached, and a wave of dizziness sent her swaying toward one of the tall-backed oak chairs by the kitchen table. She sank down, breathing deeply, helpless to stop the vision.

His head was buried in her breasts. Licking, kissing, biting, filling her with pleasure and making her clit swell.

Deft fingers moving under her waistband, into her panties, seeking her aching clit.

Pressure.

An explosion of bliss.

Mackenzie gasped, snapped back into the present, back to her big empty kitchen. Her brain hummed erratically, like the engine of her old Chevy. Her fingertips tingled.

The dull ache in her head signaled that the vision was over, and for the first time in her life she experienced disappointment at that notion. She didn't want it to end. These erotic visions were way better than the grim ones. And this one had been amazing… The feel of Will's mouth and tongue on her breasts, his fingers stroking her.

What did it mean, though? She never had visions of the past, only the future, which meant that Will's delicious exploration of her body was actually going to happen again. When? How? He'd brought someone home with him, and Will wasn't the type to cheat. He was too honorable to fuck around with another woman when he was in town with someone else.

But Mac had no doubt it would happen. The sights and sounds had been too vivid—

the scent of cotton candy on his breath, the faint melody of the merry-go-round in the distance. Whatever she'd just seen would happen at the carnival. Tonight or tomorrow.

With a sigh of defeat, she got to her feet and headed upstairs to get dressed. An hour later, she was back in her car, driving to town again.

Call her vain, but she hadn't been able to resist dressing up. In place of her usual ripped jeans and baggy sweater, she'd worn a tight, long-sleeved shirt, the same shade of blue as her eyes and with a deep vee neckline that showed a generous amount of cleavage. Skintight jeans and knee-length black leather boots showcased her long legs, and she'd even dabbed on some red lip-gloss. Her hair was loose, the way she knew Will liked it, hanging down her back in shiny waves.

He'd probably know she'd dressed up for him, maybe even take it as a sign of seduction, but she didn't care. This time she wasn't going to be caught with unbrushed hair and old sweats while in the vicinity of beautiful little Holly.

What she was trying to achieve with the get-up, she still wasn't sure. In fact, she should avoid the carnival altogether.

Yet she couldn't stay away.

He brought another woman home. You're just setting yourself up to be humiliated.

She shoved away the thought. Fine, so maybe he was seeing someone else. But she and Will had slept together last week. And they were still best friends. Holly or no Holly, Mackenzie needed to fix things between her and Will. She needed to look him in the eye and know that the sex hadn't destroyed what they had.

She also needed to tell him about the vision, the one of his helicopter crashing. Maybe if he knew, he'd stay home. He'd stay alive.

She sighed again, knowing the chances of Will not going on the mission were slim. He was a junior lieutenant. He couldn't tell his commanding officer to screw off. And even if his superior gave him leave, she knew Will would do the mission anyway. He loved being a SEAL and he took his duties seriously.

Fifteen minutes later, she reached the heart of Hunter Ridge and easily found a parking spot in front of Paula's store. Most of the other residents lived in the quaint residential streets surrounding the town; Mac was one of the few who lived on the outskirts. She liked the distance, though, the privacy and serenity of her farmhouse and rolling acres of land. Her sister Alice had left Hunter Ridge when Mackenzie turned eighteen. Alice had always hated small-town life, fleeing to San Diego the moment she didn't need to be Mac's legal guardian anymore.

Mac didn't blame her sister. Small towns weren't for everyone, and Alice's move hadn't hurt their relationship. They still spoke often and saw each other whenever they could. And when they did, Alice always made sure to chastise Mackenzie for not dating Will. Her sister was convinced—as she had been for fifteen years—that the two of them belonged together.

Letting out a breath, Mac shut off the engine and got out of the car. Maybe Alice was right. Maybe she *should* be with Will. But just as the thought floated in, a memory did too. Her last vision, the one that had finally scared Dan away.

She remembered the horror and pity on his face when he'd woken up to her sobbing and throwing up. And what he'd said…

Those words were imprinted in her brain, weighing on all the insecurities she'd felt her entire life.

I can't be with a woman like you. You represent death to me. I feel sick just looking at you.

She shoved the memory aside, but not fast enough. Her throat grew tight, her stomach churning.

She locked the car and tucked her keys into her purse, bleakly wondering if Dan was right. Did she represent death?

"Wow, you look amazing!"

Mac glanced up to see Paula poke her head out of the general store. Swallowing the pain sticking in her throat, she pasted on a smile. "Thanks, Paula. Closing up soon?"

The other woman grinned. "Of course. I plan on dominating the shooting booth tonight."

"Good luck."

"Thanks, hon. You really look terrific." Paula's face darkened. "You're not the only one, though. I just saw Will and his new flame walk by holding hands like a couple of randy teenagers."

"I take it you heard about Holly?"

Paula frowned. "They were at the diner earlier. Everyone met her."

"She seems like a nice girl," Mac said noncommittally. "Pretty, too."

"I guess," Paula said in a grudging tone. "Not as pretty as you, though. Not by a long shot."

She laughed. "Holly and I aren't in competition. Will and I are just friends, remember?"

"I guess," Paula said again. She paused. "He's never brought a woman back here before."

A lump of sadness lodged in the back of her throat. "No, he hasn't." Mac forced another smile. "I'm going to grab a bite. I'll see you later, okay?"

"Sure thing."

With a wave, Mac crossed the street and headed toward the parking lot of the bowling alley, where the carnival was in full swing. The lot was the only place large enough to accommodate such a big event, and it seemed like everyone in town had decided to make an appearance. All the rides boasted long lines, and children streaked by her, holding enormous stuffed animals and shoving pink handfuls of cotton candy into their mouths. Everyone looked like they were having a great time, but Mac only felt tense as she threaded her way through the crowd.

Paula said she'd seen Will and Holly head over here, but Mac wasn't sure she was ready to face them again. It didn't help that Holly was so beautiful. Why couldn't Will have hooked up with someone who didn't bring this funny twist of inferiority to Mac's gut?

She inhaled the scent of fried food and sweet desserts, her gaze fixed on the Ferris wheel, a commanding shape that dominated the fairgrounds. As she walked toward it, the mob parted slightly and her breath hitched when she caught sight of Will standing near the iron gate circling the ride. He was alone.

Her pace quickened, along with her heartbeat. He turned his head at her approach as if he sensed her presence. His eyes smoldered when they rested on her outfit, the tight shirt, the sexy boots.

"Hey," she said, reaching him.

"Hey," he answered gruffly.

"Where's Holly?"

"Restroom, and then she was going to make a phone call." His gaze swept over her, causing tingles of heat to spread through her body. "You look incredible."

"Thanks." She awkwardly rested her palms on her sides, then glanced up at the lights twinkling on the Ferris wheel. "Have you gone up yet?"

"No." A hint of a smile. "Want to take a ride?"

Her heart did a little flip. "Holly won't mind?"

He smiled wryly. "She's not the jealous type."

"Oh. Okay then."

They moved toward the line, but didn't have to wait more than a few moments before the passengers from the last ride were let off. Neither of them spoke as they walked up to the gate. Will watched her slide into the car, then sank down next to her, his long legs fitting awkwardly in the small space. The attendant lowered the bar and then the car soared a few feet, pausing in mid air as the next passengers were let on.

Mac didn't look at Will, sweeping her gaze over the carnival grounds and empty Main Street instead. They rose higher, and now she could see the entire town—charming houses, tidy lawns, and, in the distance, the acres of land and dusty two-lane highway that Will drove on each time he came here from San Diego. His visits had been the highlight of recent years. She always felt better when Will was around.

Pain pierced her heart. Oh God, how would she survive if he died?

"What are you thinking about?" he asked softly.

She finally turned and met his eyes, gorgeous dark eyes that could always see through her. "You. Me." She changed the subject. "So, are you serious about Holly?"

Something indecipherable flickered on his face. "I could be," he said with a shrug. "But it's too soon to tell. It's only been a week, after all."

She swallowed. "You met her the day after you left here."

He shifted his attention to the crowd below. "Yes."

"Does this mean you're—" she searched for the right word, "—*over* what happened between us?"

"Are you?"

"Yes," she lied.

His jaw tensed. "Aren't you tired of lying to yourself?"

"What am I lying about?"

"The way you feel about me."

She released a tired breath. "What does it matter now? You're dating someone else."

A glimmer of triumph. "And that bothers you."

"No," she lied again.

Will shook his head in frustration. "I can't do this anymore, Mac."

Panic tugged on her gut. "Do what?"

"Keep coming back here, acting like we're best friends."

"We are best friends."

"We should be more," he snapped, anger staining his voice. "And if you can't give that to me, then maybe it's time I moved on with my life."

She chewed on the inside of her lip. "With Holly?"

"Maybe." He made an annoyed sound. "Or maybe not. Either way, I'm not putting myself through this shit anymore."

Her panic intensified, knotting in her intestines and squeezing hard. "I knew this would happen if we slept together," she whispered. "I knew you'd leave."

"It would've happened regardless." Pain creased his handsome features. "I'm not leaving because we had sex, and it's not because I'm bitter that we won't do it again. It's just too hard, Mackenzie, wanting you this badly, knowing you want me too, and having to fight you every step of the way."

The car started its descent, and anxiety rolled through her. Soon the ride would end, they'd get off, he'd find Holly, and then he'd walk out of her life. And his helicopter would crash in the jungle, and she'd lose him for good. Forever.

Unless she stopped him.

"Will," she began.

He raked both hands through his dark hair. "Yeah?"

"I..."

I love you.

"I don't want you to go."

His mouth tightened. "Then give me a reason to stay."

Desperation rippled up her spine. She opened her mouth, then closed it, then opened it again. But no words came out. She couldn't find her voice, couldn't find the courage to tell him how she felt.

Her silence dragged on far too long. Each second ticked by painstakingly slow, and Will's expression went from impatient to irritated to resigned.

The ride came to its conclusion. A lanky teenager stepped to the platform and lifted up the bar. Without a word, Will slid out of the car. Mac trailed after him, struggling to meet his powerful strides.

"Wait," she said in frustration, latching onto his muscular arm. "I need to tell you something. Please, Will, wait."

Her peripheral vision caught a flash of red, and she turned to see Holly standing by the exit gate, clad in a filmy red dress that swirled around her thighs.

"I'm tired of waiting," Will replied flatly.

He shrugged her hand off him and marched to the exit. Holly frowned when she noticed his expression, which Mac imagined to be fierce and resentful, but the brunette didn't have time to react—in an instant, Will pulled Holly into his arms and kissed her.

Mac's heart promptly plummeted to the pit of her stomach.

Chapter Six

WILL WASN'T SURE WHY HE'D DECIDED TO KISS HOLLY. THEY'D AGREED TO some hand-holding and a few pecks on the cheek, but the anger coursing inside him like a volatile ocean current had spurred this impulsive decision. Screw Mac, and her excuses, her fear, her denial. She didn't want to give him a reason to stay? Fine, then he'd show her exactly what she'd be missing. To hell with her.

His mouth closed over Holly's, swallowing the shocked little sound she made. Carson would kill him, yes, but to hell with him too. Placing his hands on Holly's ass, he pulled her toward him, thrust his tongue into her mouth, and kissed the living daylights out of her.

His cock grew hard and his pulse quickened, but he suspected it had more to do with the fact that Mackenzie was watching. He sensed her presence, felt her eyes on him, and he knew she was still by the gate, witnessing this kiss.

To his surprise, Holly responded to him by twining her arms around his neck and sinking into his body. Her small breasts pressed against his chest, and though it felt nice, it was nothing compared to the way Mackenzie's full tits had felt on his bare chest.

Damn her.

He squeezed Holly's ass, tangling his tongue with hers, wishing it could be this simple. Kiss another woman, love another woman.

But it wasn't, and the hopeless realization that he could never get over Mackenzie Ward prompted him to end the kiss.

"I'm sorry," he murmured against Holly's lips before slowly drawing back.

She stared up at him with wide eyes and flushed cheeks. "It's fine." After a second of hesitation, she lifted her hand and touched his chin. "Are you okay?"

He practically choked on the word "No".

Holly shot a discreet glance behind them, where he knew Mac was still watching. "Let's go, then."

Nodding, he took Holly's hand and led her away, needing to get the hell out of this damn carnival. Away from Mackenzie and her goddamn excuses. He didn't look back, not even once, and when they were far enough away, he stopped walking and shot Holly an apologetic look.

"I shouldn't have done that," he said.

A devilish glint filled her green eyes. "Nope. Carson is going to kill you, you know."

Will suppressed a groan. Oh, he knew, all right. He'd be lucky if his friend didn't skin him alive.

At least Holly seemed to take it well. She'd recovered from the spontaneous kiss, the flush gone from her cheeks and a wise look in her eyes. "You're done, aren't you?" she asked quietly.

"With Mac?" Pain stung his heart. "I think so."

They began to walk again, making their way through the crowd of happy, smiling people. They reached the edge of the lot, and instead of heading over to his Jeep, he led Holly across the street. "I need a drink," he muttered.

"Me too." Holly fanned her face. "Don't tell Carson I said this, but you're a damn good kisser, Charleston."

He managed a grin. "Thanks."

She frowned. "I wish you'd given me a head's up, though. I don't kiss well under pressure."

The grin turned into a laugh. "You did just fine."

They reached the one and only bar in Hunter Ridge. A peek through the window showed the place to be practically empty, and Will held open the door for Holly, then followed her inside. He gave a polite smile to the waitress, who ushered them to a booth near the window. After they'd sat and ordered a couple of beers, Will looked at Holly and groaned.

"What would you do if you were me? Give up?"

She paused thoughtfully. "I'm not sure it's possible to give up on love."

"If Carson had put up a fight about being with you, would you have tried to force him to change his mind?"

"Yes, if I knew he loved me." Holly gave a sheepish grin. "Actually,

Carson and I were kind of in the same situation. I kept fighting the relationship and didn't want to get seriously involved, and he kept pushing until I finally gave us a chance."

"Are you glad he did?"

"Yes." No hesitation. "If he hadn't fought for us, we might not be together right now."

Will ran a hand through his hair. "So you're saying I should fight for her? Even when she's determined to pretend she's not in love with me?"

The waitress returned to deliver their drinks, and Holly lifted the beer bottle to her lips. "But you know it's a lie, and she'll admit it eventually. Because she *does* love you. You should've seen her face when the kiss ended. Sheer misery."

His stomach clenched. He did *not* like knowing that he'd caused Mac pain.

"I didn't see her trying to stop me," he finally said, then took a long swig of beer. His mouth lifted in a bitter smile. "She's probably home by now, hiding in that farmhouse the way she's done for years."

Holly's lips curved, her focus on the window behind him. "I wouldn't bet on it," she murmured.

He twisted around, his heart leaping when he spotted Mackenzie crossing the narrow street, each step she took heavy with determination. Her lush mouth was set in a firm line, her pale blue eyes flashing.

Seconds later, she threw open the door and stormed into the bar.

"You're an asshole, Will Charleston!" Mackenzie flung the insult at him like a live grenade, her cheeks burning with anger.

He lifted one brow. "Am I?"

Ignoring him, Mac turned her attention to Holly, who seemed to be fighting a smile. "You should know that you're dating an insensitive jerk."

Holly echoed Will's reply. "Am I?"

"Did he tell you he slept with me last week?" Mac demanded.

The bar grew quiet. The three patrons at the long chrome counter swiveled their heads in the direction of the booth. Even the waitress eyed them curiously.

But Mac was oblivious to the nosy stares, and that said a lot—she always cared way too much about what the people in town thought of her. "Will and I had sex last week. Did you know that?"

"No," Holly said with a shrug.

"Doesn't that bother you?" Mackenzie snapped.

"Why should it?" Casually, Holly took a sip of her beer. "If it had meant anything, he'd be with you right now, not me."

Will hid a smile.

"It meant something! It meant *everything*."

He was stunned to see her eyes fill up with tears. "Mackenzie—"

"No," she interrupted. "I don't want to listen to you anymore. I get it, you're done with me. Fine. I'm done with you too."

She spun around and hurried out the door.

"Go," Holly said with a sigh.

Will shot out of the booth and took off after Mackenzie. He caught up to her just as she reached her car. "Don't even think about running," he ordered, digging his fingers into the sleeve of her shirt.

"Leave me alone," she protested, trying to free her arm.

He tightened his grip and dragged her to the narrow alleyway that separated Paula's general store from the hair salon. A single bulb bathed the alley in a pale yellow glow, revealing Mac's wet cheeks and eyelashes that were spiky with tears. Her gaze flitted all over the place, landing on everything but him.

"Look at me," he demanded.

"No."

He edged closer, slowly backing her into the brick wall, one hand still on her arm, the other now on her chin. He forcibly made her look at him. "What the hell do you want from me, Mackenzie?"

She let out a small sob. "Nothing."

"Bullshit. What do you want?"

A few more tears spilled out of the corners of her eyes. "I don't want anything to change."

"Too bad, it has." He wiped the tears away with his thumb, then rubbed her bottom lip. "Everything changed the moment you kissed me. Not when I showed up at your house during the storm, not when I slid my cock into you, but when you kissed me."

"I already told you, I was upset about Dan and—"

"You were attracted to me," he cut in. "You're still attracted to me." He dragged his fingers along the slender column of her throat, across her collarbone, down to the enticing vee of her chest.

"Don't," she whispered.

He dipped his fingers and stroked the upper swell of one breast. "Don't pretend you want me to stop," he whispered back.

She gasped as he moved his palm underneath the lacy cup of her bra and cupped her. "This isn't right."

"It's right," he disagreed. "Baby, it's always been right."

He let go of her arm, moving his other hand underneath her shirt. He cupped both breasts, stroking, running his thumbs over her nipples. Her breathing quickened, her blue eyes darkening with arousal.

Anticipation coiled inside him, tight and urgent like a rattlesnake about to strike. With a groan, he lowered his head to those enticing tits, nuzzling one stiff nipple before catching it in his mouth and sucking deeply.

Mac gasped with pleasure.

"You like that, don't you?"

She didn't reply, only released a little moan, and it was all he needed to hear. With his tongue still licking a nipple, he slid his hands down to her ass and squeezed. His cock jerked when Mac's fingers found their way into his hair, tugging on the dark strands, keeping him trapped against her breasts. Fuck, he would never get enough of this woman.

He moved a hand to the button of her jeans, skillfully popped it open, and let his fingers go exploring. He rubbed her pussy through her panties, the heat of her searing his fingertips. His groin clenched. Fuck, he could come right now if he let himself, just from the feel of her under his palm. Mac started rocking against his hand, urging him on with soft little sounds, thrusting her tits into his face.

With a strangled groan, he shoved aside the crotch of her panties and found her clit, applying pressure with his thumb.

Mac threw her head back and climaxed, a rippling explosion that covered his fingers with moisture and made every inch of him ache with raw, uncontrollable desire.

"I'm taking you home," he ground out, barely able to breathe, let alone speak. "Right now."

She looked up at him with glazed, sated eyes. "What?"

"I'm serious, baby. I need to be inside you." He took his hand out of her panties and quickly tugged her bra and shirt back into place.

"But…" She shook her head as if trying to snap out of a trance. "What about Holly?"

It took him a second to realize who she was talking about. His supposed new girlfriend. "You don't need to worry about Holly. Just get in the car and drive home. I'll follow you there after I talk to her."

"Will—"

He cut her off with a harsh kiss, his tongue filling her mouth. Just as she began to respond, he pulled back. "Go home, Mac. And you better be naked when I get there."

MAC WAS FULLY CLOTHED WHEN WILL WALKED THROUGH HER FRONT door nearly half an hour later. During the drive home, and the subsequent wait for Will to settle things with the woman he was currently dating, Mac had had plenty of time to think and ask herself a few important questions.

The main one being, *what the hell was she doing?*

It was bad enough that she'd let Will bring her to orgasm in public, but agreeing to spend the night with him again? It was crazy. And foolish. Without the haze of sexual attraction fogging up her brain, she had a clear line of vision to the reason she'd always kept Will safely in the friend zone. Sex was temporary, but the friendship she and Will had wasn't something she was willing to give up.

And considering what she'd seen, she couldn't allow sex to complicate their fragile relationship. If he died in that crash—she refused to use the word *when*—then she didn't want their remaining time together to be messy and complicated. She didn't want to fight with him.

She wanted the familiar. Stable, comfortable Will, her best friend.

But…what if he *did* die? Shouldn't she allow herself one more night with him? She'd already decided to tell him about the vision, a goal she'd lost track of between watching Will kiss another woman and then letting the attraction distract her in the alley. She'd planned on doing it now, but suddenly she was reconsidering.

One more night in his arms, in his bed. Didn't she deserve at least that before she informed him of his impending doom?

Her heart pounded as he kicked off his shoes and shut the door. The stark desire on his face took her breath away. No man had ever looked at her like that before, as if she were his entire world.

"You didn't listen," he said huskily, moving toward her with catlike grace.

"W-what?" she stammered.

He reached her, his strong arms encircling her waist. "You're still dressed."

It took every ounce of strength to shrug out of his seductive arms. "What happened with Holly?" She kept her voice firm, determined not to let him steal her common sense the way he'd done less than an hour ago.

Will seemed irritated by the question. "I told her I was coming home with you."

Mac gaped at him. "And, what, you left her alone at Harriet's B&B, in a strange town where she doesn't know a soul? God, Will, you really are an ass!"

The callousness of his actions was just what she needed to get her brain in check. It was far easier to be angry with Will than to lust over him.

"No, I didn't leave her alone." He sighed. "Her boyfriend is on his way to pick her up."

Deafening silence filled the room.

Mac stared at him in shock, the implication of his words whipping around in her head until an uncharacteristic growl ripped out of her mouth. "Her boyfriend?" she exclaimed. "You brought her here...*kissed* her...and she's not even your girlfriend?"

"Nope."

His cavalier tone added to the jolt of betrayal in her belly. "You *tricked* me? Why the hell would you do that?"

He shrugged. "To make you jealous."

She'd known the answer before he even said the words, and she suddenly felt like a total idiot for playing right into his hands. Of course Will wouldn't have fallen into bed with someone else a *day* after he'd slept with her. He wasn't that kind of man. Will was loyal to the core, ridiculously stubborn, dead-set on getting what he wanted, and for fifteen years, he'd wanted *her*. So much so that he'd resorted to juvenile tactics to get her.

And he'd succeeded, that son of a bitch. Mac knew without a doubt she wouldn't have let him touch her in that alley if Holly hadn't been in the picture. The sight of Will with another woman had made her insane with jealousy and driven her to give Will exactly what he wanted.

"Oh, don't look at me like that," he said dryly. "You would've done the same thing in my place."

"Maybe in the *sixth grade*," she huffed. "Damn you! It's not fair to play with people's emotions like that."

He moved closer again, the spicy, masculine scent of him filling her nose and weakening her resolve.

She held up a hand. "Don't you dare come any closer. I'm furious with you."

Another shrug. "Good. Angry sex can be damn hot."

She swatted at his outstretched hands. "I'm not having sex with you."

"Yes, you are." His voice was smoky with heat and seduction.

Almost immediately, her mind cleared of everything but the desire she felt for this man. She forgot about the vision of his helicopter, her anger about his lie, everything.

Damn it, she wanted just one more night with him.

Mac's muscles clenched in anticipation as he thrust his hand in her hair and angled her head to accommodate his approaching mouth. The kiss was electrifying, molten hot and deliciously erotic. His tongue pried her lips open, delving into her mouth and flicking determinedly against her own tongue.

Then his lips moved, and he was exploring her neck, nibbling her flushed skin. "You are going to have sex with me," he rasped. "Tonight, tomorrow morning, tomorrow night, and the night after, and the one after that. I'm going to fuck you every second of every fucking day, until you won't remember what it's like not having my cock inside of you."

She whimpered.

His mouth returned to hers, his tongue tracing her lower lip. "Now take off your clothes. I want to look at you."

She feared he might've cast a spell on her, because she found herself doing precisely what he'd asked. She stripped off her shirt and bra, then wiggled out of her jeans and panties. Just like that. He commanded, and she obeyed. She should hate herself for her weakness, for how easily she gave into this man's husky orders and persuasive hands.

Will's dark eyes studied every inch of her exposed body. Each time his gaze lingered, flames licked at her skin. She was unbearably hot. Painfully aroused.

Damn him.

Features strained, Will unceremoniously ripped his shirt over his head, then tackled his jeans. After he'd shucked his boxers, he stepped toward her. Naked, beautiful, his cock jutting out eagerly.

Moisture pooled between her legs. She wanted every inch of him buried deep inside of her.

"Spread your legs," he ordered.

She did as he asked, shivering wildly as he sank to his knees and kissed the inside of her thigh. His big hands rested on her butt, drawing her toward his waiting mouth.

Mac threw her head back and cried out when his tongue found her clit. The sensations swirling through her body were too much, too fierce and too hot and— "More," she gasped. "Give me more."

He did, burying his face deeper, sucking harder on her clit until she couldn't stay upright anymore. He tugged her down to the floor and repositioned her so that she lay flat on her back, legs wide open, her pussy exposed and aching for him.

"You're so fucking beautiful," he said gruffly. "I want to eat you up, baby."

"Do it then." The bold words slid out before she could stop them.

He gave a faint half-smile and dipped his head. Her hips surged toward him, and she rubbed herself against his mouth, desperately taking every bit of pleasure he had to offer. He brought his tongue back to her clit, licking gently, while two long fingers worked their way inside her hot channel. The resulting orgasm sent a bolt of lightning up her spine, seizing her body and lighting it on fire.

She heard her moans fill the room, but the reckless, blissful sounds seemed to be coming from far away. All she could hear, see and feel was Will, and his tongue, his fingers, his hot breath on her clit.

Mac barely had a chance to come down from the orgasmic high

when Will grabbed a condom from his discarded jeans, climbed up her body, and drove his cock inside her. There was nothing gentle about his movements. The hardwood floor beneath her back was cold and unforgiving, but it only added to the rising urgency, the rough, unrestrained thrusts and desperate groans.

It had never been like this with any other man. So good, it was so damn good. Her arms tightened around his muscular back, nails digging into his sinewy flesh. Will let out a harsh curse, muttering, "Too fast," even as he was shuddering over her, jerking wildly as he came.

His breath came out in pants, his shaft pulsating inside her, and Mac found herself smiling as she looked up at his sexy, dark eyes. She liked seeing Will lose control. He was always so serious, his emotions never quite reaching his eyes, but not now. Now, she could see everything he was feeling. The raw desire, the tenderness, the love.

Love.

The notion made her stiffen, but Will quickly captured her mouth and kissed her. "No," he ordered against her lips. "You're not pulling back from me again."

She tried turning her face away from the possessive kiss, but he wouldn't have it.

"No," he said again, and before she could blink, he withdrew, lifted her to her feet, and carried her into the bedroom.

Chapter Seven

IT ONLY TOOK TWO DAYS FOR WILL TO ACCEPT THAT HE WOULD SIMPLY never get enough of Mackenzie. He wondered, as he strode out of the bathroom on Sunday night, if this was even natural. He and Mac had stayed in bed since the night of the carnival, only getting up to grab a quick bite or take a shower, though both activities had resulted in yet another round of hot sex.

The only downside was that he sensed there was something on her mind. Every now and then she'd grow silent, bite her bottom lip, or look at him with a troubled frown. He hadn't pushed for answers, though. The last thing he wanted to do was remind her of her previous reservations about him. About them.

"Your phone rang again," Mac told him as he resettled on the bed.

Her raven hair was tousled, and the sight of her rosy cheeks brought a smile to his lips. She'd come only moments ago, and he loved seeing the remnants of climax on her flushed face.

Drawing her warm, naked body toward his, he absently stroked her bare shoulder as he reached for the cell phone sitting on the dresser. The missed call was from Carson.

Will sighed.

Next to him, Mac peered at the phone and laughed. "Oh, call him back already. He can't kill you when you're here and he's all the way in San Diego."

"Wanna bet?"

"At least check your messages, then. Maybe he's not even angry."

"Again, wanna bet?"

Still, he punched in the code for his mailbox, then pressed the speakerphone button. A moment later, they heard Carson's voice.

"You kissed my girlfriend? My fucking *girlfriend*? I don't give two shits if you're my superior. I'm kicking your goddamn ass, Charleston!" *Click.*

Will glanced at the naked woman in his arms. "See?"

"Let's hear the next one," she said with a laugh.

He hit *delete* and moved to the next message.

"Holly just told me you had your hands on her ass. I swear to God, I'm tearing your throat out." *Click.*

"Had enough?" Will grumbled, about to toss aside the phone.

Laughing uncontrollably, Mac grabbed the cell from his hands. "One more," she begged.

Carson's voice again. "Okay, I may be starting to calm down. Holly just reminded me that I fucked my best friend's wife not so long ago and—"

"What?" Mac's eyebrows shot to her forehead.

"—a kiss isn't as bad as sex. Nevertheless, asshole, it's still pretty bad." *Click.*

"He had sex with his best friend's wife?" Mac demanded.

"Threesome," Will answered, as if that explained everything.

"Okay." She studied him curiously. "Have *you* ever had a threesome?"

"Nah, I'm a one-woman guy." He grinned. "I'd rip the head off any man who tried to touch you in front of me."

"Interesting. I'm in bed with a barbarian." She tilted her head. "Does that mean I can rip Holly's head off?"

He snorted. "Not unless you want to contend with Carson. Besides, that kiss meant nothing."

She narrowed her eyes. "So you didn't get hard?"

Will shrugged.

"You did!" she exclaimed, jabbing an accusing finger into his bare chest. "I can't believe you!"

"I only got hard because I knew you were watching," he admitted sheepishly.

"Even when you knew it was driving me crazy with jealousy?"

Another shrug.

Mac's lips curved in a devilish smile. "I think it's time for some payback."

"Oh really?"

"Mmm-hmmm." She shoved away the sheets tangled between their bodies and straddled his lap. "Maybe it's time I drove *you* crazy."

"Baby, you drive me crazy just by breathing."

Still, her wicked threat had intrigued the hell out of his cock, which was now harder than concrete and jutting out hopefully. Mac grinned when her gaze landed on his erection. She reached down and circled her fingers around the base of his shaft, tugging gently.

A shudder wracked through him. "I was about to make us some dinner," he protested.

"Ha! Your cooking is as bad as mine. We'll order pizza after I'm finished with you."

Despite the fact that he'd fucked her, oh, about five times today, his arousal levels skyrocketed. The tip of his cock tingled, anticipating Mac's next move.

Her next move consisted of sliding down his chest and taking him into her mouth.

Heat speared into him. His balls tightened, his muscles grew taut. He would never tire of this woman. She was fucking incredible. Her mouth was hot and wet and tight, and he groaned as her tongue teased his cock. One hand pumped his shaft while the other cupped his balls, fingernails scraping over the aching sac.

Will moved his hands to her hair, stroking the silky strands and guiding her head over him. It was hard to control himself, to stop from thrusting deep into her throat as far as his cock could go. His pulse pounded in his ears, pleasure sizzling through his bloodstream as the hot suction of her mouth and insistent strokes of her hand brought him closer and closer to the edge.

His cock demanded to be inside her, to feel her wet pussy fisted over him, but Mac refused to release him. Her mouth devoured him, making its own demands, until the pleasure was too much and he came in her mouth.

Heart pounding, he sucked in a lungful of oxygen, wondering how she did this to him. Made him lose control every damn time.

"Okay, we're even," she teased, kissing his tip quickly before rising up on her knees. Her bare breasts were tinted red with arousal, but before he could reach for her, she swatted his hands away. "Order that pizza, Charleston. I'm hungry."

"Fine," he grumbled.

He dialed the number of the one and only pizza place in town and placed a quick order. He was assured the pizza would arrive within half an hour, and he couldn't stop a grin. Thirty minutes was plenty of time to make Mackenzie come again. But just as he'd hung up the phone, it rang again.

Rolling her eyes, Mac remarked, "Mr. Popularity."

He glanced at the screen, then stifled a groan. "Fuck."

Concern filled her eyes. "Who is it?"

"My commanding officer." Letting out a breath, he answered with a curt, "Charleston." He listened to his CO's brisk orders, hung up, and released another breath, this one tinged with regret. Raking his fingers through his hair, he glanced at Mac. "I have to go."

The concern in her gaze was joined by a flicker of panic. "Why?"

"The team's been called. We're flying out tonight."

Since they'd been in this position a bunch of times before, him getting called out while visiting her, the horror that widened her blue eyes shocked him. He instantly sank to the edge of the bed. "Hey, what's wrong?"

A shaky breath flew out of her mouth.

"Mac, talk to me. What's going on?"

She stayed quiet for so long he began to worry, and just as he was about to pull her into his arms, she spoke.

"Don't go."

She sounded so agonized, he wondered if he was missing something. "What?"

"Don't go," she repeated, her shoulders shaking as she sucked in a gulp of air. "Please, Will, you can't go."

MAC'S HEART THUDDED SO LOUDLY SHE COULD BARELY HEAR HER OWN voice. The entire weekend, she'd tried not to think about the vision. And it had worked. She'd spent the past two days in Will's arms, kissing him, making love to him, laughing with him.

She'd been wrong when she'd thought sex would complicate things. If anything, she'd never felt closer to him.

But those awful images—the smoke, the helicopter—had lingered in the back of her mind, reminding her that any minute, any second, she could lose him.

She'd thought about telling him, but she hadn't wanted to spoil this perfect weekend. Now, she couldn't hide from it anymore.

Tears welled up in her eyes, and her throat was so tight she couldn't get any words out.

Will had her in his arms in a flash, his hand delicately pushing her hair away from her face. "It's okay," he murmured. "Tell me what's wrong."

She finally lifted her head. "I don't want you to leave me."

His dark eyes softened. "I thought we got past this already. I told you, I'll never leave you. I love you. You need to believe that."

"I do believe it," she whispered, swiping at her wet cheeks. "This isn't about…that. It's…please, Will. Don't go on that mission."

A heavy silence fell. She could feel his gaze on her, could practically hear the puzzle pieces snapping into place in his mind.

In a low voice, he said, "You saw something."

She drew a ragged breath. "Yes."

"Involving me."

"Yes," she said again.

He swallowed, his throat working hard. "How bad?"

"Really bad."

A tear slid down her cheek. Instantly, Will's thumb wiped it away. She met his gaze, surprised to find it calm and steady, as if what she'd just told him was no big deal.

"What is the matter with you?" she demanded, the panic returning to her chest. "Didn't you hear what I said?"

"I heard."

"Then why are you so calm?" A thought suddenly occurred to her, bringing a rush of relief. "You're not going. That's why you're not freaked out. You're going to stay here."

"No, I'm going."

Her head snapped up. "No. You *can't*. You'll die."

"Did you actually see it? Did I die in the vision?"

Helicopter falling from the sky, hurtling toward the canopy of green below.

"I saw…your helicopter was shot down," she said slowly.

"Did you see my body?"

"No, but—"

"People survive helo crashes all the time, baby. Your vision doesn't have to end in death."

His unruffled composure infuriated her. "You *can't* go."

"It's my job," he said quietly.

"Screw your job! What about your life?" Her breaths came out in sharp pants. "What about everything you're always saying to me, how you'll always be there, how I won't lose you?"

"I've always meant what I've said." He reached out for her, but she shoved his hands away. "Come on, don't be like this. I'm a SEAL, Mac. I deal with dangerous situations all the time, and I always come back."

"You're not invincible. What if you don't come back this time, Will?"

"Then I go to the grave the happiest man alive." He shot her a crooked smile. "I just spent the weekend with the woman I love."

Her hands began to shake. "Stay with me. Please."

He sighed. "Mac, this is my job. You've always accepted it before."

"Yeah, when you were my best friend, not the man I lo—" She halted.

Will's dark eyes glimmered. "Finish that sentence."

"Only if you promise not to go."

"Finish the sentence."

She fought another wave of tears, her heart squeezing so hard she thought it would stop working altogether. "The man I love," she choked out. "There. After fifteen years, I've finally quit being a coward and said it. I love you, Will. I love you so damn much and I refuse to lose you."

Pleasure shone on his face. "I love you too. And you won't lose me."

"If you go—"

"I have to go," he cut in. "Being a SEAL is who I am. It's a part of me. Just like the visions are a part of you. They make you who you are. I accept that, and you've got to accept this."

Her chest ached so badly it felt like someone was scraping it with a dull blade. Will shifted, and the next thing she knew he'd flipped her over. She lay on her back, with Will propped up on his elbow next to her, gazing down at her with gorgeous black eyes. "I love you,

Mackenzie. And no measly helicopter crash will keep me from coming home to you."

She closed her eyes. "If something happens to you..."

"Then it happens." He placed his palm on her stomach and traced her belly button with his fingers. "Which means we need to take advantage of the time we have now."

Her breasts began to tingle as his fingers drifted toward them. His touch was warm, gentle, and her body swiftly responded. Nipples hardening, clit swelling. It bothered her that she could still get turned on when her entire body felt bruised, when her stomach still churned with the fear of losing him and the anger that he was putting himself in the position for that to happen.

She intercepted his hand before it reached the swell of her breast. "I was wrong," she said shakily.

His forehead wrinkled. "About what?"

"You." When a frown creased his mouth, she hurried on. "You'll always be there for me, won't you?"

"That's what I've been trying to tell you all along."

Then he framed her face with his hands and took possession of her mouth, his lips firm and reassuring. The kiss brought the tears back to her eyes.

She loved him. She had always loved him. She'd never felt like she'd truly belonged until Will moved to Hunter Ridge. And fifteen years later—God, how had he waited this long?—fifteen years later she was finally ready to admit it. Admit how much she wanted him, needed him.

As if he'd read her thoughts, he moved over her body and rubbed her opening with the tip of his cock. "Let me in, baby," he muttered.

Since she'd already widened her legs, she knew he wasn't talking about sex. It was hard to form a coherent sentence when he was stroking her like that, teasing her clit with his cock, but she managed. She moistened her suddenly dry lips and said, "I love you."

His breath hitched. After rolling on a condom, he pushed his cock inside her and then he began to move. At each thrust, she neared the edge, close to toppling right over it. She wrapped her legs around him and dragged her fingers up and down his back.

He captured her lips with his and quickened his pace. Faster. Harder.

Until her body quivered beneath his, her inner muscles squeezed against his dick, and a wild moan flew out of her mouth. She came hard and fierce, her heart thumping in her ears. Will let go a moment later, his cock jerking inside her while his lips stayed pressed to hers. Mac gripped his neck and pulled him closer, relishing the feel of his fast heartbeat against her breasts.

"I love you," he said hoarsely, burying his face in the crook of her neck.

Slowly, he withdrew, then wrapped one muscular arm around her waist and pulled her closer. They lay there, silent and sated, until finally he disentangled himself from her embrace and sat up.

"I have to go now."

Tears pricked her eyelids. "I know."

He rose from the bed and began gathering up his clothing. She said nothing as he dressed, just watched him through a sheen of tears. God, let him be okay. Let her vision be wrong. For the first time in her life, just let her be wrong.

Sliding his cell phone into his pocket, Will approached the bed where she lay tangled in the sheets, her body still feeling the effects of him.

With a sexy smile, he bent down and kissed her. She responded frantically, kissing him back so hard she was almost embarrassed. But he didn't seem to mind. Their tongues dueled, breaths coming out heavy, and then he pulled back.

"I'll see you soon," he murmured.

Her chest throbbed with pain. "Promise?"

"You fucking bet I do."

Smiling through her tears, she watched him walk out the door.

Epilogue

"So…let's not do THAT again," Carson remarked dryly as the chopper approached the helipad at the Coronado Naval Base.

Will managed a shaky chuckle and glanced around the small space, assessing the other men. Like him, they were covered in mud and reeked like the swamp they'd crawled through for ten hours. Garrett had soot on his face from the explosion. Ryan Evans' right arm was bandaged from the bullet that sliced through it. But other than that, they were all in good shape.

He experienced a flicker of pain as he thought about their pilot. Craig hadn't survived the crash. Fuck. Will didn't want to be there when they told the guy's wife.

"I'm still pissed off that you knew this would happen," Matt O'Connor grumbled, giving Will a dirty look. "Some warning would've been nice, Lieutenant."

"You can't change the future, man. Telling you guys would've achieved nothing."

Ryan cocked his head, looking intrigued. "So your girl really saw it happen? She saw the crash?"

Will nodded.

"Think she knows who I'll be screwing tonight?"

He rolled his eyes. "You were shot in the arm. I doubt you'll be screwing anyone."

Ryan looked at Matt and grinned. "He underestimates my sexual prowess."

As the pilot set the chopper down, Will noticed Carson glaring at him. "What now?" he asked the other man.

"Just thinking about how you kissed my girlfriend, that's all."

"Seriously? How many times do I have to apologize for that?"

"At least, oh, about a thousand more."

Garrett jabbed Carson's ribs. "Hey, you *fucked* my wife. The LT's a choir boy in comparison."

The chatter died once the helicopter landed. The men immediately jumped out, and Will watched in amusement as his teammates took off. Carson and Garrett moved the fastest, obviously eager to wash the mud off and go home to their women.

Which was precisely what Will planned on doing.

Striding into the building, he headed down the corridor and walked into the first empty office he saw. He made a beeline for the phone and dialed so fast he hoped he hadn't pressed the wrong numbers.

But then he heard her voice.

"Hey," he said gruffly.

There was a stunned silence, and then, "Oh, thank God! You're okay!"

He fought a smile. "Is it inappropriate to say I told you so?"

"Very." There was a soft sniffle. "I've been going crazy with worry. Your commander called when you lost radio contact and he sounded freaked, and… Oh God. Are you sure you're all right?"

"Yep. In perfect health, too." He wrinkled his nose. "I smell like shit, though. I should probably hop in the shower before I—"

"Don't you dare," Mackenzie interrupted. "You're to do nothing but get in your car and come home."

"It'll take me some time to get there. You'll have to exercise some patience, baby."

"Don't talk to me about patience. I've spent the past three days waiting by the phone."

"Well, sit tight for just a while longer. I'll be there soon."

"Will?" Her voice shook. "I love you."

His heart did a dumb little flip, but, fuck, he loved hearing those three words come out of her mouth. "I love you too, Mac. Always have, always will."

"Good. So come home, Will. Now."

He grinned. "Yes, ma'am."

The End

About the Author

A *New York Times*, *USA Today* and *Wall Street Journal* bestselling author, Elle Kennedy grew up in the suburbs of Toronto, Ontario, and holds a BA in English from York University. From an early age, she knew she wanted to be a writer and actively began pursuing that dream when she was a teenager. She loves strong heroines and sexy alpha heroes, and just enough heat and danger to keep things interesting!

Elle loves to hear from her readers. Visit her website www.ellekennedy. com, and while you're there sign up for her newsletter to receive updates about upcoming books and exclusive excerpts. You can also find her on Facebook (ElleKennedyAuthor), Twitter (@ElleKennedy), or Instagram (@ElleKennedy33).